AND BREATHE

Leonora Meriel is the author of four novels. Her debut work *The Woman Behind the Waterfall* was hailed as "strange and beautiful" by writer Esther Freud, "a literary work of art" by Richmond Magazine and "an intoxicating world" by Kirkus Reviews. Leonora studied literature at university and lived in New York, Kyiv and Barcelona before settling in her native London. She has three children. Read more about her life at www.leonorameriel.com.

ALSO BY LEONORA MERIEL

The Woman Behind the Waterfall

The Unity Game

Mbaquanga Nights

AND BREATHE

LEONORA MERIEL

GRANITE CLOUD

Published by Granite Cloud 2022

ISBN 978-1-915245-04-5

Cover design by Anna Green

To Valentina, my constant inspiration

AND BREATHE

DAY ONE

Laeticia

VIPASSANA.
Sssshhhhh.
Peace.
I am Laeticia.
Palm trees. A hornbill screech. Juan's face.
Three hours of silence before breakfast.
Ten days of silence after breakfast.
Breathe.

It happened two years ago.

I didn't tell Juan about it. He was away in San Sebastian for two weeks, perhaps already with *her*. I was pregnant, although I hadn't told him yet. I thought I would lose the baby. I thought I would have a disease.

It was in Paris, walking back from the café after a late closing, and there was someone behind me – the clicking of expensive shoes approaching, the biting scent of a strong aftershave. An arm went around my waist. Not softly, but hard, locking my body into its grip. I looked up towards him in panic – a mistake maybe? Could I push him away? – but he was walking forward with purpose, only now with me, unable to get away, beside him.

I glanced the other way, my panic increasing. Even at that point, there was no doubt in my mind as to his intention, as to what would happen if I didn't extract myself from the situation. I'd always thought of that street as safe, busy at night, but right then, there was no one. Perhaps a face in a lit window? He must have seen the opportunity.

I remember the light as orange, but Paris has the white and yellow lights, so it must be my memory colouring the scene. I'm putting the Rio de Janeiro lights onto Paris, although Rio was never dangerous for me. I would know what to say to someone in Rio to make them run. But in Paris, I didn't understand the motivations deep enough.

"My husband is waiting for me," I said, trying to pull myself out of his grip. It wasn't true. My husband was in San Sebastian, possibly with his mistress. "I'm pregnant," I said, short of breath now. It felt like I wasn't drawing enough oxygen into my brain to say the right thing, to fill my limbs with the strength they needed to act. He was dragging me into the outer courtyard of some buildings.

Why didn't I scream? I was sending commands to my throat, to my mouth, to my legs, but they seemed to have shut down. I could feel my heartbeat, but the rest of my body had stopped responding. It had closed off, disassociating itself from what was happening. *You're on your own*, it was saying.

"Beautiful, beautiful," he whispered. *"Ma belle. Ma belle,"* as if it was a romantic evening, as if I'd been gazing at him over a candlelit dinner with a red rose in a vase for hours. And then it was happening. *Ma belle.* The aftershave. The pain. His expensive shoes.

Then he was gone. And I felt betrayed not by him, or men, or the Paris police, but by my own body. Why had it let me down when I needed it the most? What was the point of being able to run for miles in the Bois de Boulogne or along the Barra da Tijuca if I could not run when I was in danger?

My legs were so weak I felt drunk as my steps weaved home. I climbed the stairs to my apartment, locked the door behind me, then lay down on the floor in the corridor. I thought of all the women in the world who had ever been raped. I thought of all the women who had been raped that very day. *My* rape day. I thought of my mother. I wondered if I was going to lose the baby.

Breathe.

Perhaps every woman has this day. Perhaps when we're born, we have a day we're going to die, a day we will give birth and a day we will be raped.

When I worked for the UN Refugee Agency, I dealt in the statistics of sexual assault. In some conflict zones, there was a twenty-five percent risk of an attack taking place, regardless of age. Nonagenarian, baby, it didn't matter. If you were a woman, every morning was a day that your turn could come.

So, I'm in good company. I think about the women who've been attacked by soldiers in their burnt-out houses, after having seen their children killed in front of them. And I wonder what they would say if I asked them whether they would have preferred to be assaulted in a medieval courtyard by a well-dressed Frenchman smelling of eau de cologne. Would they laugh and spit on me? Would they look at me through dead eyes? Or would they take my hand and say, *yes, we are family?*

Breakfast time. Mounds of dragon fruit, mango and melon in colours of sunset. Piles of lychees, pineapple, papaya.

I queue up with the women. The men have their own entrance to the dining hall, separated by a wooden barrier. We can see the jungle through the glass walls. I bite into sweet pineapple and my body tingles as I look out at the layers of green on green. After breakfast, we embark on our mandatory stroll along the boardwalks and set paths outside. I stretch my legs as I walk; long, low strides. The air is warm and wet. I tense all the muscles I can, then relax them. The men have their own routes. There are many rules here. No jogging. No yoga in the rooms. No talking to the men. No scented face-creams. No pens or paper. No music. No clothing that reveals too much flesh. No food except for what is provided in the dining room – *simple vegetarian*, as the booklet describes it. No phones, no technology, no visitors. No leaving the grounds, no running into the jungle, no quick smoke late at night.

And most important of all: no speaking.

They say that in the first seventy-two hours, the mind will create a furnace of thoughts and try to force us to say words, any words. But once it learns that the barrier of silence is impenetrable, then a window to peace will be opened.

Low resonance of a vibrating gong. We are being called back to the hall. I inhale the jungle air once more, and then exhale slowly. I am ready to meditate.

The end of the first day. Eleven hours of observing our breath.

In the final hour, a video was played to the room of worn-out meditators. S. N. Goenka, the man who fulfilled a 2,500-year-old prophesy to bring the meditation technique of the Buddha back to India, appears to us, dressed in a white gown. His face is laughing and empathetic. His words are kind and humorous. He tells us that we must be tired. He tells us that these ten days will be arduous. He tells us that we can escape from pain and suffering.

I picture students sitting in meditation halls around the world, listening to these videos, seeking an escape from pain and suffering. Yet it seems to me that more than this we are seeking a pause from the insanity of the world raging unstoppably around us. A single, long moment of calm, untouched, while the mass of endless information piles higher and wider, continually rendering our lives smaller and more displaced and stripping away levels of reality and connection and serenity and any time – any real time to process any of it.

Perhaps, as our world continues to whirl faster, these meditation centres will be the only place left where time can stop; where breath can ease; where minds might rest.

Breathe.

"Will I ever get over it?"

I had finally managed to ask the question. Anabel and I were sitting at a corner table of my arts café, Si La Femme. She'd been helping me run it for the last few days.

Anabel had flown over from New York as soon as I told her what had happened. She just packed a bag, went to the airport and got on a plane. That's the friend she is.

She'd never been to Paris before but she fitted right in. She matched sharp New York business suits with heels and a foot-high afro and even the Parisian women gave her jealous looks, which is the greatest compliment they have to bestow.

"I feel unsafe everywhere," I went on. "I see men as threats. I feel physically vulnerable. My body carries fear. If I see a painting of a man and a woman, I see only danger."

Anabel reached across the table and took my hand. She was a straight talker. She never softened blows.

"You might not get over it," she said. "It was a serious assault. It'll take a lot of time and work." She paused to let me digest what she'd said. "But we're not afraid of hard work, right?"

I shook my head. We were both hard workers.

"And I'm here to help you. We'll keep on it 'til we get there. However long it takes. Could be boxing, self-defence, group therapy – whatever fixes it, we'll find it."

"Okay," I said. It was about as much as I could say. I might not get over this. Something had been done to me and I might never get over it. That was terrifying.

"Laeticia…" Anabel was giving me her power look. A beam of pure strength that took men down and raised women up. "Listen to me. We're on this."

Breathe.

Ivan

Bloody mosquitoes.

There's one biting my neck right now.

Smack!

Got the bastard.

I am Ivan.

Three hours until breakfast. My stomach is roaring. I've lost two kilograms already. How many vegetables can a person eat?

Blood pressure. It's going down. Less panic.

Zhenia's face. Again. Blood pressure rising. Heart is racing. I'm going to pass out.

I can't take revenge if I'm dead from a heart attack.

I've been to Thailand before. I don't remember there being any mosquitoes on Phuket Island, though. I recall a lot of sashimi and fantastic service and truck loads of fruit. I lost some kilograms then as well. Eva told me I should come here – she'd heard something about it. "You're going to die," she kept telling me. "You're going to have a heart attack. The pills aren't doing anything."

After Zhenia tricked me into signing documents and I was voted out of the company with a diluted share price, I went through three stages. The first two weeks I couldn't eat. I felt like I was floating. My body and mind rejected all food and drink. The only thing I could get down me was *kefir*, unpasteurised, fermented yogurt. Zero fat *kefir*. Maybe it isn't even a food, that's why my body accepted it, but I lost five kilograms in those two weeks. I spent the days wandering around the city. I had known Zhenia since I was five. We were in kindergarten together, we were in school together, we stole companies together in the '90s, we grew rich together. We trusted no one – not our wives, not even our children. But we trusted each other.

He has to die.

The second two weeks I smoked non-stop, so my diet became zero fat *kefir* and cigarettes. Eva was going nuts, of course. Her money supply had been cut off. She was thinking about the children's school and the teacher bribes we had to pay; she was thinking that her friends now had better handbags than her; she was thinking that if she stopped her cellulite massages then she'd get lumpy thighs. Or maybe I'm wrong. Maybe she was just worried that I'd have a heart attack and she'd be left penniless. Maybe she was figuring a game plan. I hope so. She might need one. Smart girl, Eva. She'll make sure the children are alright. I wonder if she ever slept with Zhenia.

In fact, now I'm sure of it. If Zhenia betrayed me in this way and manoeuvred me out of my own company, then why wouldn't he screw my wife? And it would be just like Eva to sleep with both business partners, in case one goes down.

Are my children really mine?

The mosquito has bitten me again; they probably carry diseases. They should spray these places before they let people in. The new bite is itching. I can feel it swelling. I've got to scratch it. *Blin!* Dammit! There's another one. The person beside me keeps turning round; he's making a hissing sound. He can get lost. I can't sit here for ten days if I'm going to get eaten alive. That wasn't part of the deal. It's just a bit of scratching.

Observe the breath, they say. Breathe in. Breathe out. Honestly, I could have done this in Kyiv.

"You've got to go," Eva had said. "Otherwise, you will fall dead in front of me. Then what do I do? What about the children?"

She had wheedled my doctor into agreeing as well. "Ivan," he said, "Vanya, she is right. I gave you the strongest pills I can prescribe and they are not working. Your stress is too deep."

"Give me something stronger," I told him. "Don't prescribe it. Just get it for me."

"That will be an even faster way to die," he told me.

I was pacing the living room floor. Eva came in with a cup of coffee for the doctor.

"Boris, you've got to tell him. He's going to die." She started crying those ridiculous fake tears. She was probably thinking about the new shoes she couldn't buy or the cancelled trip to Milan.

"I'm not going to spend a fortune going to some remote jungle and sitting in a filthy room for two weeks," I shouted.

Eva flashed a look at me. One of those triumphant, teary ones when she's got what she wants.

"It doesn't cost a thing," she said. "It's free. You just pay for flights."

"What do you mean it's free? I won a prize, did I?"

"Nobody pays," Eva said. "It's a system. People who do this meditation think it's so good they pay for someone to go on the course after them."

"So, I pay later," I said.

"Not if you don't want."

"No. I *don't* want."

And that's how I ended up in this room.

Then the third phase hit me: resignation.

Zhenia, Zhenia, Zhenia, Evgen, Evgenii, Zhen, Zhenichka, Zhenia.

We met when we were five, at kindergarten. We were dropped off by our grandmothers. Mine was large and solid, like a tank; his was strong and wiry, like a sniper gun. He pinched my ear, I punched him in the stomach, then we rolled on the floor, delighted to find a commensurate amount of rage and desire for violence in each other. When they pulled us apart and sent us to different sides of the room to be surrounded by groups of girls, we were alive, grinning, elated.

Zhenia. My best friend. My partner. The witness at my wedding. My thief-in-arms.

I will miss him when he's dead.

Breathe, they say. Breathe.

I breathe. I am breathing.

Focus on the breath, they say. Let the thoughts pass. Just observe the breath.

Okay.

Here are the thoughts I am going to let pass:

Different ways to murder Zhenia.

The possibility that Eva is sleeping with Zhenia.

The possibility that Zhenia is the father of my children.

The possibility that the takeover was plotted by Eva and Zhenia, and that when Eva persuaded me to come to Thailand and not look at my phone for ten days, she was planning to move in with Zhenia and arrange for me to be arrested and sent to prison when I get back.

The possibility that the doctor is in on it too.

The possibility that my mother has heard everything and has died from the shock.

The possibility that my children are now calling Zhenia *Tato* – Father.

The possibility that I'm going to die from a heart attack in the next week. My blood pressure will go up and up and up, and my arteries will explode from rage.

The possibility that the whole business community now knows how I have been betrayed and duped and sent away and are drinking vodka and laughing until they cry at what a fool I am.

The possibility that I will be assassinated at Bangkok airport on my way back.

The possibility that Zhenia will have paid off my bodyguards and that they will take me out when I arrive home.

The possibility that Zhenia has got the mother, wife and daughter of one of my bodyguards locked up and won't free them until I'm taken care of.

The possibility that even if none of that is true (and most of it probably is), I will be penniless when I return and embroiled in dozens of court cases filed by corporate wolves trying to get money off me, and that Zhenia will have paid all the judges in advance to rule against me.

The fact that now Zhenia is gone, I have no one in the world to trust or to tell my thoughts to.

The fact that my heart hurts every time I think of it and feels like it will burst open and blood will spill out.

There. These are the thoughts I will let pass.

No problem at all. Let's just give them a tidy sweep. Let's get the broom and pan and *one, two, three*, we're done.

What a waste of time. I'm hungry. I want breakfast. They said there's no meat here. How am I going to get through two weeks with no meat? They searched my bag when I arrived. It was a circus. They laid it all out on the reception table: mobile phones – three of them; a radio; four packets of meat; aftershave; computer; some Valium, sleeping tablets. No vodka, though. Eva must have gone through my bag in Kyiv and taken the bottle out. Sneaky bitch. I should have eaten the meat in the taxi. I made them promise to put it in the fridge. First thing I'll do when I'm finished here: get my meat back.

They say that some famous oligarchs do this – silent meditation retreats. They come and spend ten days in the jungle every year and it gives them vision. Who told me that? The doctor, maybe? Or I read it somewhere. It's the young ones, I'm sure, not my generation. Our meditation is meat and vodka. Our meditation is the sauna and crayfish. Our meditation is three strippers and a kilo of black caviar.

At least I don't need to sleep yet. It's four-thirty in the morning here, that's eleven-thirty at night in Kyiv and I'd usually be at the nightclub now, sitting at a table, drinking vodka. There'd be some friends, some business partners, some girls with legs at the bar, maybe one on a pole. It's like I always say – no real business gets done unless there's a girl dancing round a pole in the centre of the room. Not in Kyiv, anyway.

There. I feel calmer. I'll ignore all the other thoughts and just focus on one. A lovely girl around a pole. Long legs, high heels, red thong, naked breasts, rubbing that pole, rubbing, rubbing...

Smack!

Bloody mosquito.

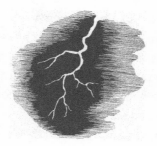

Francis

Four-thirty a.m.

Ten-thirty at night in Paris.

I am sitting cross-legged in a silent meditation hall in the middle of a Thai jungle.

A fan is creaking as it circles on the roof above us.

A small animal is scampering over the tiles.

I hear the heavy breathing of the man on my left.

I smell the toilet soap of the man on my right.

The person behind me has shifted position five times.

I am Francis. I am François.

My job is to anticipate future risks to my country.

But I reached the point where all I could see was risk.

A short break, they said, *to calm your mind.*

Vipassana.

Everyone feels better afterwards.

We will be waiting for you, Francis.

Don't come into work tomorrow, Francis.

See you in a month, Francis.

Goodbye. Au revoir.

Good luck.

I took the bus from the local airport. Thirty meditators cramped together, wiping the steaming windows for a view of the Thai landscape: jungles and distant mountains, villages and perched temples. I sat beside an Englishwoman who was returning to "serve" for the ten days. While we meditated, she would be cooking our meals and cleaning our showers, washing the dishes and beating the gongs that would wake us up at four in the morning. I liked her. She was excited about ten days of hard, menial work. I was moved.

"What has brought you to Thailand?" she asked.

"My head," I replied, "gets fizzy. I see too many things. I observe too intensely. I cannot switch my mind off and then my reality becomes distorted." I paused. "Or so people tell me."

She laughed. "The main principle of Vipassana is to observe intensely," she said. "So, you should be great at it."

Her words didn't make me feel good. Her words made me worried.

On the first evening, having settled into our rooms, we trooped into the meditation hall where we would spend eleven hours a day meditating, a hundred and ten hours in one space, two feet by four feet, our small place of peace. We listened to the instructions.

They were simple: Observe the breath. Release any thoughts that draw your focus away from it. Do not breathe deeply or strongly. Breathe through the nose, as if you were not paying attention to the process. Observe the movement of the breath in and out of the nose. Do not follow it down to the lungs. Do not track its passage out into the meditation chamber. Just the small movement in and out of the nose.

Simple. Specific. Seriously impossible.

"Close your eyes. Observe the breath."

The time is four-forty-five. There are ten-and-three-quarter hours remaining to observe the breath. It is not going to be any different. I have observed it. It is shallow: low intake of oxygen, release of carbon dioxide.

If there was a chemical attack on the meditation centre and we had to seal the room with no air coming in, I calculate how long we would survive. Eight cushions by eight cushions: sixty-four cushions on the men's side and the same on the women's makes one hundred and twenty-eight. Teachers at the front, a row of old students and monks down each aisle give an extra twenty. One hundred and forty-eight people in the room.

I estimate the volume of the chamber, with twenty percent oxygen content and net consumption of four cubic metres an hour. Divide this between a hundred and forty-eight people and we have fifteen days to survive.

However, in the case of an attack, we'd be in fight-or-flight mode with a double respiration rate. That takes us to seven-and-a-half days. And the meditators would be dying off, with the corpses using oxygen to decay, so let's deduct two days for that. Oxygen only needs to decrease to ten percent of air composition to induce coma and death, so we're down to three.

Three days, then. If there is an attack and we need to seal the hall, then we're all dead in seventy-two hours.

If we were to draw this on a chart, we'd use Time as Axis X and Panic Level as Axis Y and I'd draw the oxygen as a line steeply descending, hitting the horizontal at three days, to show total death.

However, this also supposes that the hall can be properly sealed. We have dozens of thick blankets for us to wrap ourselves in while we're meditating, and I'd help them secure the doors and windows, but if the gas or chemical was strong enough then it would seep in, and we could all be dead within an hour.

Unless there was a strong wind.

Another graph: Strength of Chemical meeting Wind Level. Lay on top of that the percentage of success in sealing the hall windows and doors with blankets. Then the wind level seems to be the dominant factor. But who would launch a chemical attack in a high wind? Someone of low intelligence. So, another variable: intelligence of the attackers.

New graph: Intelligence of Attackers on Axis X, Wind Level on Axis Y.

These are both random factors over which we have no control.

So, in the event of an attack, the main factor of survival is chance.

How is this helping me be calmer?

I am meant to be breathing.

I should take in as little oxygen as possible, just in case.

"I like your accent," the Englishwoman on the bus had said. "You're French?"

She was pretty. She was wearing a cotton dress to her knees, and no make-up. Her hair was in a ponytail. But it wasn't a case of having no sense of fashion or making a statement by being pared-down. It just felt natural. I was drawn to it.

"I'm both French and English," I replied. "A father of one, a mother of the other."

"Where did you grow up, then?" she asked.

"In English boarding schools and French farmhouses," I replied. But that sounded pretentious, so I added, "and a poky Paris apartment."

"I'm from Liverpool," she said. She just offered it. Like the dress and the clean face, it was a simple statement. I began to wonder if I'd met anyone else like her. I knew plenty of women who dressed badly and wore ponytails, but I got the sense that she could have been all sorts of interesting things, and she was *choosing* this clean simplicity. But then I don't trust my senses anymore. They tell me too many things that start my brain fizzing. *I'm from Liverpool*, she told me. No more, no less.

"Francis," I said, holding out my hand.

"Jo," she replied.

"Or François, if we're in France." Again, I sounded pretentious. Her clear eyes were bringing out the fool in me.

"Two names," she said, with a little smile. "That must get confusing."

"My mother called me Francis, and my father François. In France one, in England the other. Not confusing at all."

We laughed.

"I should start calling myself Josephine when I go to France," she said.

We said goodbye when the bus pulled into the jungle clearing. She went off with the group of servers and I remained with the meditators. First task: lock away all electronics and writing materials. I sent a final text to Jimme before I switched off my phone.

Arrived safe. See you in 11 days. Enjoy the flat. Remember to lock the door. F.

Then I sent another one.

I love you. F.

A heaviness rushed suddenly into my head as I locked my phone away for good. And then a flash of hope: what if my mental state had been caused by the negative impact of technology and endless information? Technology was the greatest security risk to the world, central to all the terrifying scenarios I had mapped out for my department. Could locking my phone away help me?

Then I remembered once again that *no*, it was not technology that had caused my unbalanced mental state. It was moving to

England to work at Hartbridge Laboratories. And a science fiction teacher. And reading science fiction books.

I walked away from the locker, trying not to let my mind begin running down those paths. I could see it warming up, stretching, ready to begin a powerful, stamina-heavy journey into the terrors of the surrounding world.

I did not cry.

I was in a place that might be able to help me.

I looked around instead. A jungle of intense lime green. A rustling noise coming from the distance. Hot, thick, rain-tinged air.

DAY TWO

Laeticia

BREATHE.
New day.
Empty mind.
Juan's face.
Anger rising. Juan's eyes. Juan's mouth, on me, *on her!*
Breathe.

"Perhaps after this meeting I could take you for a coffee," he said.

It was not the most inspiring chat-up line. We were in the middle of a United Nations sustainability session. He was outstandingly handsome amongst the grey suits, and he knew it.

The dark brown hair, the eyes full of intelligence and romance, the expensive clothes – scruffy, but from making love and staying over, not from needing to buy an iron. I knew I was the obvious choice. When you're a slender, six-foot Brazilian it's hard to hide from men's attention, even in business dress. We were the obvious couple to go on a date.

I never liked to be obvious.

"I have sessions with the women leaders booked all afternoon," I said. I looked him full in the eyes, just so he knew what he was missing. "There are women all over the world who need our help right now."

"There are different needs that require different kinds of help," he replied. He gave me the look back, so I would know what *I* was missing.

"There are different ways of satisfying those needs," I said firmly.

I knew I had him there.

I was working on a task-force to rehabilitate survivors of sexual assault in conflict zones. That was in the morning. Then we had a report on cooking stoves in rural India. I was heading up some of the sub-groups. Juan had nothing to do with the women's projects. He was with the Argentinian delegation and had been wandering around looking for something to do.

He was one of those men to whom everything came easy: school grades, jobs, promotions, women, money, apartments, good health, exceptional physique. It was a level of entitlement so deep the entire world had melded itself around his desires.

I, on the other hand, representative of ambitious women everywhere, was passionate, dog-working, got nothing for free, watched every calorie, was careful with my investments, took only the most calculated risks and knew that everything could be snatched from me at a moment's notice. Because it wasn't my world yet – it was his. But I was fighting to make it mine.

I didn't plan to fall for him. I didn't usually go for privileged types. But it was so easy. We went dancing that night and I remembered all the fun I used to have in Rio, before New York imposed its work-only ethic on me. His life was laughter and pleasure. Being with him was looking at life as a playground of infinite fun. Life for me was a mountain and I was halfway up it, wearing the latest climbing gear and with my axe stuck in the frozen rock. Each move had to be examined from every angle or I would plummet to certain death. I was alone on that mountain.

Then I took his hand and loosened my axe from the rockface. His lips on me. His lips on *her*.

I plummeted.

I went to the doctor after it happened. I was fine. I was checked for everything and the baby was not affected – not physically. Yet my daughter had experienced an unthinkable trauma before she was even born. How could that not affect her? She had my terror running through her unborn form. She had the full emotional spectrum of the event passing through her. Would that make her afraid? Would it make her angry? Would she have a subconscious need to repeat those emotions?

Her father is a liar and a betrayer, an anachronistic pillar of male privilege. Her mother is taking on the burdens of the world and making them her own, carrying them up the mountain. She is bearing a legacy I hoped she would be free of. She was born into a world I was trying to change so that she would not know these things.

Beatriz.

She is my daughter.

I left her with my mother in Rio. So, while I am here, purifying my memory of male-inflicted traumas, her young mind is being filled with the impressions of a good Brazilian woman: boiling rice, stirring beans, washing all the pots and pans, mopping the floor, sweeping the dust, brewing coffee, feeding the cat, walking to the market for fruit and vegetables – and all the while the good Brazilian man is sitting in the comfortable armchair reading his newspaper.

"Bring me my coffee, *querida*," he says, and my mother brings it.

"More sugar, *querida*," he says, and she adds it.

"Stop fussing, Maria, you're making me dizzy," he says, so she cleans in another room.

I started counting, when I was with Juan, the number of things I did compared to him. In the morning alone, I would go running in the park, shower, arrange my hair and make-up, dress smartly, tidy the apartment (because I like it tidy), shop for food, make breakfast (only for me), and answer some e-mails. This was before Juan even woke up, an hour and a half later. I calculated that on an average day, I would do three times more work than him.

How do we make things equal? The divisions run too deep. Where can I take Beatriz so that she will grow up knowing that society is fair? Do we have to live in Reykjavík? Or Stockholm? Maybe that is the answer.

Breathe.

They said the first few days our minds would be in chaos. But I need peace!

"There is another woman," he said. He was back from San Sebastian.

Quite separate from the barrage of hurt I was feeling, I was genuinely interested if he was ashamed or regretful. I had known about the other woman. I had made plans. I had attached new climbing ropes to my harness. I was trying to decide whether to tell him about the pregnancy. Or about being assaulted while he was away. I could knock him off his see-saw. I could send him flying down the slide and onto the gravel. I could push him on the roundabout until he went frog-green and vomited.

Tell him? Not tell him? Hurt him? Yes! Give him access to my pain? No! Give him a chance to know about his child? Yes? Have him possibly hanging around my life forever with his life-affirming laughter and happy eyes? No!

"Yes, I know about that," I said. I watched his face. There was a hangdog sadness that looked like cheap play-acting. "I want you out of the apartment."

"I'm moving to San Sebastian," he replied.

"I don't want any details," I said. "I want you gone."

So he left.

We had moved from New York to Paris a year after our marriage. I had a dream of opening an arts café where I would host political meetings. I had enough experience and contacts to hold events that would have an impact, and I wanted to get away from the convoluted structures of the UN and do it in a more creative manner. I could host exhibitions and artists, speakers and music. I had more in my soul than just statistics. There are many ways to change the world.

I did it. I polished my French and arranged a loan from the bank. I was picturing Anaïs Nin huddled in a corner, falling into conversation with Nathalie Clemont, the UNHCR Congo specialist who had been my friend in New York, with the Toulouse Gypsy Swing Band playing in the background. Music and political thought and activism and intense writing and great coffee all mixing together in a swirl of Paris life. I opened the café. It was perfect.

Juan had got himself transferred to the Argentinian embassy.

He was working relaxed nine-to-five days with long diplomatic lunches near the Jardin de Tuileries. In true form, I was up at six every morning for a run, opened the café at nine, then managed it and planned events until we shut at eleven in the evening, or later if we had music and dancing. Juan would often come to the café to eat, with his diplomatic friends.

And now, if he comes back to the café one day and I am there with Beatriz, what will I say? *This is your daughter. I was raped when I was pregnant with her but I didn't tell you because you were in San Sebastian cheating on me with another woman.*

Or, I could say: *this is your daughter, but you have no right to be in her life (assuming you would want to be) because you betrayed me and lost the place by my side.*

Or, *yes, you are the biological father of my child. If one day she asks about you I will explain to her why you are neither in my life nor hers. But until then, I would like you to leave.*

Or, *yes, she has your eyes and will grow up with some of your grace and intelligence and natural happiness and laughter. But she will also grow up knowing you for your ability to take from the world with both hands and give nothing back.*

Why do women do this? Why do we picture the man returning and asking for forgiveness? They never do.

Breathe.

Ivan

Twenty-six.

That's how many mosquito bites I have.

Arms, hands, legs, neck, face.

They can smell weakness, I'm sure. Zhenia cut me open and now they smell the blood. I don't see anyone else scratching. I'm clearly an easy target, close to death.

I slept like a baby last night. Six hours cold. At ten p.m. we were sent to bed like *shkolniki* – schoolchildren – and at four a.m. the gong started ringing. It's something, at least. In Kyiv I don't think I'd slept for weeks. Not from the moment I found out.

And in yesterday's meditations I kept falling asleep. I was good for the first couple of sessions, but once it hit five a.m. Kyiv time I started snoring. The Thai fellow next to me put his hand on my shoulder each time I dozed off. It was strange, but I didn't mind it. Normally I'd have shoved him away, but he just looked like he didn't care at all; he was doing it to help himself and help me. Neutral. Maybe I'll punch him later.

Now, let's get back to why I'm here. I'm here so that I won't die. I'm here to get my blood pressure under control. I'm here to get some calm so I can make a strategy to return and take Zhenia down. Good. All good reasons. I'll give it a day, then I'll see what my nice, calm mind comes up with. Murder him first then take the business? Or take the business and let him die from unhappiness? No, that's what he's trying to do to me. He could just come here and meditate and get better. It's got to be more final.

At least it doesn't smell of feet in here. I was imagining a hundred yoga-meditators with unwashed hair and clothes, and noxious feet, but it seems good and clean. The meditation hall is white and peaceful, with blue cushions in rows for us to sit on. They're telling us to sit in this pose that Eva uses when she's doing her yoga, but my legs don't bend like that. I'm just cross-legged. With the cushion, it's easy enough.

The people here don't look too bad either. A lot of Thais. A few foreigners. One girl looks South American, a real beauty. I haven't caught her eye yet. They have us sitting on different sides of the hall – there's a white line down the middle to separate the men and women. I'll find her somewhere later.

Now. Scratch. Then breathe.

Nice.

Scratch.

Stop scratching.

Now legs are itching.

Now face is itching.

Now the man next to me is looking. Not the neutral one from last night. This one looks annoyed. I'd happily push him. I've just got to scratch my neck first. Now arms. Now hands. *Aaaaaah.* The bites are red and throbbing and pulsing and itching like mad. I've got to scratch them all at once. I've got to tear them, rip them, destroy them. *Aaaaaaaah.*

There. I've got one. I've taken one down and it's bleeding all over the place. It was a big one on my hand. It's getting all over my white Adidas. Damn. How do I stop it? There's another one bleeding now, on my arm. *Blin!* It's getting all over my sports trousers. I look like I've been shot. Like I'm bleeding from my chest and my legs. So, this is what it will be like! How much longer in here? I've got to get out. I've got to eat something. I've got to wash off this blood and put on some new clothes. I'm going to die! I'm going to die! Oh my god, I'm crying now.

Come on, Ivan. Breathe. Breathe. Get the air in. Get the air out. Just stop crying. Then stop bleeding. Just stay alive for the next hour. Can I do that? Mama's voice: *Ivanushka, Ivanushka. Lie down and sleep.* There. I'm calming down. Or something better. Kotik's voice: *Vanechka, lie down and close your eyes. I'm going to make you feel so hard, baby.* Oh, God, Kotik was so good. Will I be able to afford her anymore? Has she heard? Of course she's heard. I haven't called her. She'll have found out why. Will she see me again? She doesn't like losers. I can text her. First thing I'll do when I get my phone back. I'll text Kotik. I'll buy her a gift. God, I miss her. Nobody can make my cock feel as good as she can. It's okay. Calm down. There. Now I've got a nice erection. I'm bleeding, crying and I've got an erection.

I'm getting better by the minute.

I've had a lecture from the teacher. They let me have breakfast first. The *kasha* wasn't bad and the fruit was pretty good, even though I hate fruit. The teacher came to me – one of the ones wearing orange sheets. Teacher, monk, I don't know. He took my arm where I'd been bleeding and wiped it with some disinfectant and wrapped it with a strip of cloth. I didn't mind him. He was like the one last night, who put his hand on my shoulder to wake me up. I don't feel I want to push these ones, it's like they don't have masculine energy; I don't feel any urge to hit them or drink vodka with them. They're just kind of genderless. Anyway, he wasn't saying anything but he wrapped up the wound and then he put both hands over his heart and he was looking in my eyes and nodding, and he made gestures to breathe, so I did it with him. I breathed with him, and then I put my hands over my heart, like he showed me, and we breathed, and then I noticed that I was crying again. He made a gesture like this was okay, so we sat, and we breathed, and I was crying and then he nodded and we stopped.

He brought me some tissues and made that praying-bowing movement, and I felt like at that moment he was my only hope in the world, and I wanted to hug him and hold him to me, but I thought this would probably upset him, and then I'd lose my only hope, so I did the praying-bowing thing back, and he left.

I was alone in the dining room by then, so I blew my nose for a while and stopped crying. I had a couple of minutes to get to my room and put on some new Adidas. I've got ten suits, so I'll be fine. I glanced in the mirror when the gong went for the next session. I was a mess. I didn't look so furious anymore, I had this pathetic, hurt, scared look. It's a stage, of course. I need to get the hurt part out of the way and cry my eyes out before I can come through and get my head ice-cold clear. That's when I'll be able to make a decent plan.

But for now, it's just me sobbing away with my orange monk.

I miss Kotik.

It was the happiest of times.

Zhenia and I were laying the foundation stones for our new mansions. We'd bought plots of land in Koncha Zaspa, the most elite part of Kyiv, where multi-million-dollar palaces nestled among pine woods. If you're wondering where Ukrainian tax-payers' money went in the '90s, Zhenia and I used to joke, just take a drive along the road through those woods. You'll glimpse underground garages and swimming pools, helicopter pads and marble columns.

Anyway, it was our turn to build and we'd hired Italian architects to lay out our houses. We'd brought along a

Ukrainian Orthodox priest in a tall, square hat to bless the land, as well as a couple of loaves of bread and some rough salt. Zhenia had a bottle of vodka and I had four shot glasses.

We arrived at the first property – mine – and piled out of our Bentleys. Eva was there, on her best behaviour, and looking ridiculously sexy. We weren't married yet and she was determined to make that house hers, so it was happy-happy time for Ivan. Zhenia was holding Katya's hand like it was an iron clamp, which pleased me, because in my book, the tighter you have to hold on to someone, the closer you are to losing them. Katya was looking beautiful with her mounds of blonde hair piled and wound around her head like an Italian peasant; breath-taking as usual. Between Eva's dark eyes and black, sleek hairdo, and Katya with the golden haystack hair, we had the most beautiful women in Kyiv. We knew it, too.

The priest was sprinkling holy oil, blessed in Jerusalem and flown in for the ceremony. Zhenia poured out the vodka. It was horseradish-flavoured *samohon*, home-made by a neighbour in our village. It was our little tradition for the moments that were really important to us. Going back to the roots.

We lifted our glasses. Zhenia and I put our arms around each other's shoulders. We had tears in our eyes. We had made it.

"To us!" I shouted.

"To us!" Zhenia echoed.

A vision of our vast, marvellous mansions rose before us: pink marble, white marble, excess in every direction. It was too beautiful for words.

We drank.

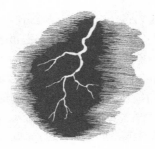

Francis

Four-thirty a.m.

Ten-thirty at night in Paris.

I am not sitting in a local bistro with a plate of snails roasted in garlic and butter and a glass of crisp, dry Chablis.

I am sitting with my back straight and my legs folded over each other and my abdominals tensed and my eyes closed. I am observing my breath.

No. I am *thinking* about observing my breath. I should be observing my breath. I have the entire day to observe my breath. I have until nine o'clock this evening to observe my breath, which is sixteen-and-a-half hours. So, no, I am not observing my breath. I am thinking.

It was all fine when I worked in Paris.

They came to find me when I was still at university. A letter – so mysterious! – asking me to come to a pub in Cambridge on a particular evening.

"We would like to invite you to work with the Direction Générale de la Sécurité Intérieure," they said. "The DGSI. We have a contract ready for you. Start date as soon as you graduate."

And there it was. Recruited by the French equivalent of MI5 before I turned twenty-one. I was given an apartment in the sixth *arrondissement* bigger than my parents' pied-à-terre, and began work in the scientific laboratories that anticipated and prevented security attacks on the French nation, its territories and allies. It sounded daunting at first, but it was quite a logical process: if these people are able to make these weapons of destruction from these materials in these places, then what might other people make from other materials in other places? And how might we a) stop them; b) best react to them by saving people in the case of not stopping them; and c) identify signs that they are in fact preparing these weapons.

It felt good. Often we were right, and we had some notable successes and visits from the Élysée Palace. Hands were shaken. Shoulders were clasped. Tears were shed. A certain number of people were alive who wouldn't now be alive, due to our work and our minds and our laboratories.

But then my superior came to see me one afternoon. "We have agreed a programme with Britain," she said. "We are exchanging personnel for a temporary secondment. We have decided to give them you."

I was shaken by the phrasing of it: *nous avons décidé que c'est vous qu'on va leur donner. I* was seen as something to be given. Something belonging to them that could be retained or discarded as they wished. It shook my sense of self as a French hero. After that, I was quite pleased to return to my other country.

Hartbridge Laboratories.

Hidden in plain sight in an ugly London suburb, a department ten times the size of the Paris one. A laboratory superior even to the Cambridge research facilities. Colleagues so busy and intelligent, they made the French scientists I had recently left seem like a group of friends chatting over a long lunch break.

Among others, we had a team matching UFO sightings with Chinese hypersonic rocket technology and updating our own in-progress rocket designs; we had teams on chemical weapon attack antidotes; and a team preparing for extra-terrestrial contact scenarios.

Flash-forward two years and I was huddled in a corner of the main laboratory, shaking uncontrollably. I was cold, freezing, and someone had wrapped a blanket around me.

"It's alright, Francis," a voice was saying. "It's alright. We've phoned a taxi. Take nice, deep breaths now."

"The trouble with you, Frenchie, is that you're always in two places at once."

Hilary called me Frenchie, refusing both Francis and François.

"This is nonsense, Hilary. I am here, right now, with you."

We were drinking beer in the Emmanuel College bar. Hilary was studying Classics and was bizarrely passionate about it. We had met in Freshers Week and she had decided I would be her lover. "I don't want to just sleep with humanities men," she had explained. "I need to try out all the different types while I've got the chance. Also, you've got the sexiest accent.

"You have two names," she continued, as usual ignoring my interjection to follow her original point. "You have two nationalities. I know you like men as well as women – don't deny it. You're clever enough to get a double first in your finals. Even your college has two names – Gonville and Caius. Everything with you is in twos."

"But I am still here, right now..." I attempted to hold my point.

"And that gives the impression that this is your fundamental nature." She picked up the pint glass and drank a third of it. "I think that you can't function as a singular entity, but that in any situation you are present only so far as you are also present in another, parallel situation."

"Is this philosophy or science?" I asked, sipping my ale.

"It's psychology," she replied.

"Perhaps it's an advanced state of being," I suggested, and immediately regretted it. It was a schoolboy thing to say.

"I like it," Hilary said. "It's no criticism, Frenchie. But it's important to know yourself, isn't it?"

"Or *yourselves*, in my case," I quipped.

"I've got it!" she said. "A double agent. A spy. An undercover life. A wife and a mistress. Or a husband and a lover. A government job by day, an erotic dancer by night."

Hilary downed her pint. The front strands of her hair had somehow got dipped in the beer.

"You exist, and will exist, in a state of duality," she said. "I think that's cool."

"And you?"

"I'm far too excitable to be duplicitous!" she said. "When I find something I really like, I can't think of anything else. My entire system is taken over, starting with my mind, then my heart, then my body. Like how I feel about you," she said. "And Sophocles."

At least I was in good company.

"Duplicitous," I said. "I don't think this is the correct word. This does not describe the state of duality."

"But it will always be lurking there," she said. "The potential for duplicity. The dark side of your nature. It will be calling you."

She laughed and stood up, tucking strands of beered hair behind her ears. "I'll get you another, Frenchie," she said. "Then let's go back to my room and unify that duality of yours."

"Can you say that in ancient Greek?" I asked, tilting my head provocatively, but she had already taken the glasses to the bar, and in any case, it was horribly pretentious.

. . .

Hilary, like me, had attended a single-sex boarding school, so when we met there was a sex-starved teenagerhood to make up for. We both had some encounters to boast of, but neither of us had experienced, as the students would say, *on-tap sex*. It was a fantastic feeling, bustling from lectures to laboratories all morning, and then tumbling into bed with a plump nineteen-year-old at two in the afternoon, before going for beers and then home to sleep. Hilary was direct and passionate and irreverent and funny and intelligent and she took me as a package of positives and negatives, which was a relief. It wasn't mindless love, but there was vast warmth and even vaster lust. We could go two or three times, sleep for an hour, then head out for a stroll. We might be working for exams, but she would come to my room and insist that I take her against the wall, and then she would leave without even removing her shoes or her clumsy jumper. It was never boring. Dear Hilary. It was never boring.

This morning, after breakfast, waiting in my room for the next meditation session, I run my mind over the meditators I have observed, committing them to memory. We're not meant to look at other participants, but my brain demands that I gather information before it can quieten and feel safe. I conjure an image of the meditation hall. To my left, a small Thai man with an old face and a child's body. Thin, hairless limbs, smooth hands, the smell of soap. To my right, a Canadian. Clean, wrinkled T-shirts and a man-bun. There may be a toe ring. He breathes heavily and has an earnest look to him. Behind me is the one I think of as *the fidgeter*. American, it seems to me. Every thirty seconds he is scratching, coughing, yawning, changing position or sniffing. Beside him, at the edge of the line, is the sobbing giant. Everyone in the room has noticed him. He's dressed in the largest, whitest tracksuit I've ever seen. Yesterday the whole hall heard him sobbing. I think we were all trying to figure out what had made him break down, and what our own break-down points might be. Will we all be sobbing by the end of the course? Will I be next? I wouldn't be surprised.

In front of me is the strangest figure in the room. Tall, thin and dressed in an ankle-length sackcloth robe with a hood so deep you can't get any glimpse of the face. The robe is tied at the waist with rope, and the sleeves are so long even the hands are hidden. I can't be the only one conjecturing about who is concealed in there. Someone deformed? That was my first guess. Then I thought, someone famous, a singer, an actor. Or someone rich and recognisable. Then I went darker, to the sackcloth. A murderer repenting. Someone wanted by the police. A fugitive.

Across the white line, the women's section is a canopy of black hair with an occasional blonde or orange frizz twisting among it. One woman on the edge stands out, her height and grace making it hard not to be drawn to her. Short dark hair and dark skin – something unpredictable about her. I imagine a great strength within, something that could uncoil.

And finally, my roommate, Tor.

"Is there anything I should know?" I asked him on the first day as we unpacked. We had a couple of hours before the silence began.

"I don't snore," he said solemnly. "You?"

"No," I answered.

I placed my alarm clock and water bottle on the bedside table between us and folded my T-shirts onto the shelf.

"Spiders," he said.

I turned to him. He was pointing at the ceiling above the door, where a six-inch arachnid was poised in a web.

"You're scared of them?" I asked.

"Help me," he said.

There was no chair to stand on and we had taken an oath not to kill, so Tor went in search of a cup. He returned with a plastic pint glass. Standing on the bed, I caught the spider and slid the Vipassana rules booklet over the top – the only paper we were allowed. Tor eagerly took the glass and disappeared from the room.

What I didn't say to him: sometimes I wake up in the night screaming, sometimes weeping, sometimes shaking. I despair of humanity. Sometimes my mind is a glass bowl, in which all the potential threats of the world are swimming, and they are so thick that I can't see anything beyond the reflected curves.

But no, I don't snore.

DAY THREE

Laeticia

BLUE CUSHION.
    White room.
    Breathe.

The white line separating the men and women is a comfort to
me. If only this white line was everywhere in relations between
women and men. If you want to cross over, you ask permission.
Better still, you go to registration and get an official document,
stamped and approved by the administration and the person you
would like to address. Then there will be no doubt whatsoever.
You can look and smile and talk and flirt all you want from your
side of the white line. But if you're planning to come over and

start touching another human being, you can do the paperwork. Married or not married? Number of sexual partners? Number of sexual partners abandoned? Number of sexual assaults? Number of STDs? Number of STDs passed on to other partners? Specifics of STDs? And I'm not just talking about men. There are women who should fill out this paperwork. In fact, everyone should fill out this paperwork. Yes. References from previous partners. Number of times you have walked out of a bedroom satisfied and left the other one with no orgasm. It would be great to see a woman reading those statistics. Here we have a charming, funny, educated fast-talker. Let's for the sake of argument, call him Juan. He is attractive, successful, amusing, arousing. Now, paperwork please.

Women Slept With: 367.

Women Abandoned: 89.

Women Caused Pain To: 218.

Percentage of Times in Bed When Both Parties Come: 10.

STDs: 1 identified.

STDs Given to Other Women: 25.

Hmmm. *Wipe that smile off your face, Juan. You're not getting any more sex. Not until you can improve those statistics.*

And my statistics?

Men Slept With: 35.

Men Abandoned: 15.

Men Caused Pain To: 10.

Percentage of Times in Bed When Both Parties Come: 95.

STDs: 0.

However much you like a bad boy, the thought of visiting the doctor and a lot of itching is going to turn off even the most eager woman.

The statistics can eat you alive, though. When I got the job at the UN Refugee Agency my first project was investigating the numbers.

Women's section. Sexual assaults in conflict zones:

Hundreds of thousands of cases per year. Actual numbers: 50,000 in Bosnia. 250,000 in Rwanda. Too many to even count in the DRC.

You sit in an office and these numbers are milling around you, and the walls of your security are suddenly thinner than you thought; in fact, they are transparent – no! no! they have disappeared! Gone are the smart clothes that signify a well-paid job in a respected establishment. Gone are the multiple degrees in languages and foreign relations that led you here. Gone is the police force that protects citizens. Gone are the guarantees that you are respected and protected. Suddenly, those walls are no more and you are flesh. You are a pillar of warm flesh. Anyone who wants you will take you. They will come with weapons. They will come with physical strength that you cannot match. They will come with superior fighting skills that your fiercest struggle cannot overcome. They will knock you down and take you as a pillar of flesh. And you will say: *But these clothes cost two thousand dollars and I have a post graduate degree and speak four languages and live in the safest city in the world.* And they don't need to reply, because they have just burned down your house and taken your children away, and they have ripped the clothes from your body.

The statistics in Brazil alone: 100,000 women raped every year – and they are the ones reported. Over half of that number aged thirteen or younger. The numbers were always alive for me. I recorded these statistics and I knew that I wasn't safe. I knew that if we lived in a world where these numbers could be written down, then this was not a world that was safe for me.

Blue cushion.
    White line.
    Breathe.

. . .

When I met Juan, I was being eaten alive by those statistics. Working with the women's groups who were on the front lines and making recommendations for decisions that would not provide enough support in any scenario, however much I recommended. Dividing up funds that were so far short of adequate that it was laughable, weepable, screamable, smashable – how many words could I come up with for the fact that I was sending a few thousand dollars to help a group of women who would take a lifetime to recover and would never, ever, live in safety? It made me shake with panic and fear for them.

Then, Juan. Simple. Handsome. His world a beautiful playground. He was life itself in all its grace and effortless abundance. He said, *We can live. Say yes to living.* And I said, *Yes.* He said, *Marry me.* I said, *Yes, yes, yes, yes, yes.*

Would you have assaulted those women, Juan, in a different life? Would you have walked into their hut in an army uniform and set it alight? Would you have dragged out the girls you wanted while other soldiers were killing their children?

What stands between you and them? You take what you see. You take what you desire and you walk away leaving their homes burning.

I do not know where the boundaries are. All I see around me is betrayal. My own betrayal, mirrored in the betrayal of all women over all the world. Women owned by husbands and fathers. Women denied education. Women denied healthcare. Women denied legal rights. Women denied the same salaries as men. Women denied promotions. Women denied the integrity and safety of their own bodies. Everywhere I turn I see pain. I see women being raped in a multitude of different ways.

And now I have a daughter who I am bringing up in this world. She is at home right now with my mother, learning inequality and sexist mores. What should I teach her? Should I teach her the anger that I carry? Should I teach her to be wary of all men? Should I teach her self-defence? Self-defence for toddlers? What can I possibly teach her except the opposite of what the world shows her? *They say you are a valued human being, darling, but it is not true. You are seen as an object for male consumption; everything you do will be treated with less respect than anything done by someone with a penis; you will never truly be safe in your body unless you carry a gun and know how to fire it quickly.* And if I don't tell her this? Then I am lying to her. I am condoning and excusing the situation in the world by pretending it does not exist.

It's a fucking joke. I didn't even study feminist theory. I was not a feminist. Was not, am not. I studied languages. I studied foreign relations. I moved to New York. I won the job at the United Nations. But in my office, the statistics came to life around me and I travelled to those countries. The women in those statistics invited me into their lives and I went. They showed me what had happened, they stood beside me and pointed. I looked, and then I looked around my office and around my country and around the planet with different eyes. *You have our numbers*, they said to me. *You have our lives. You have enough power to do something. It is in your hands now.*

That was when I joined the ranks of unsmiling NGO workers. I had laughed at them before, with my friends from the international relations course at Columbia. And now I knew why it was so damn hard to get a smile out of any of them.

Oh, I was ripe for Juan.

Breathe.

"My god, I thought you were so serious!"

Anabel was drenched in sweat and her low-cut dress was clinging to her. We stumbled out of the Rio nightclub we'd been dancing in since midnight, and I took her hand to lead her to the beach. It was nearly sunrise.

"I *am* serious!" I started to laugh and guided her across a road. She was weaving chaotically. "First and second place, huh?" I said. "We couldn't get those if we weren't serious."

Anabel paused to high-five me. We'd just finished the first year of our degree at Columbia and we'd hit the top two spots in the end-of-year exams. We'd studied together all semester, so I figured we deserved a weekend dancing in Rio. I bought the tickets as a surprise.

"No one serious dances like that," Anabel was half-shouting, though I'm not sure she was aware of it. "And why the hell did you leave Rio when there are men that hot who dance like that? What's wrong with you?"

We reached the beach and stopped to take off our shoes. The sand was fine and crisp against our toes, and the vista of wide, white, sunrise-lit sand stretching into the dark ocean was intoxicating. Why had I left Rio? I'd never asked myself the question directly. I'd always been focused on the next goal. It was the natural way to live, in my mind. Achieve, reach. Achieve, reach. Onwards and always up.

"Brazilians can do that," I said. "Dancing and partying and life on the beach is what we do. But the smart people still go to university and get great jobs. I've always worked hard. But I've had some hot boyfriends too."

"Hot, hot, hot," groaned Anabel.

"It's just our culture," I went on. "We grow up with music and dancing and festivals. It's the way we live. Like you've got your traditions – your fireworks on the Fourth of July, your Thanksgiving."

"I'd give all that up for caipirinhas on the beach," Anabel shouted. "Let's find some Latin bars to go dancing in New York."

"They won't be as good as this," I laughed. "But you're on. And Rio's always here for us."

"Anytime we start getting burned out with studying or jobs, let's do it," Anabel said. "There's a world to change out there, but I don't want to miss out on life while I'm changing it."

"It's a promise."

Ivan

I slept so well last night. I thought I would be tearing my skin for hours and cursing, but I just lay down on the tiny bed in the narrow room, pictured the orange monk and passed out.

Now, to focus. If I'm going to kill Zhenia, I need to know why and how he did what he did.

We last went out to dinner together about a month ago. *Tsarskoe Selo* – the Tsar's Village restaurant. We were in a private corner where we couldn't be seen by the other diners. We each had a bottle of vodka in front of us. We had plates of *salo* – raw pig fat, and pickled cabbage, some herring and fried potatoes. Just simple food. We laughed. We talked about the business.

"It's going great," I said. "It's shitting cash like a herd of cows."

"The workers want more money," Zhenia said.

"How badly do they want it?" I asked.

"They're going to strike," he replied.

"Then we should do something bold that will make them remember," I said. "It's a good opportunity. Let them strike, then fire all of them. Every single one. Have a couple of them beaten up, maybe even killed – separately, I mean. Like in the town, not at the strike. Nothing to do with the strike. Then, when they come begging for their jobs, we offer them back at lower pay."

"It's a good idea," Zhenia said. "What if they don't want to come back? What if they refuse to work or find other jobs?"

"What other jobs?" I asked.

"Good point," said Zhenia.

The town where we had our factories didn't have any other sources of employment. Many of the Soviet-era plants across Ukraine had closed and people had been forced to leave, to look for new work. It was a problem. The workers knew it was a problem. But the factories were so inefficient – others, I mean. Somehow, ours were still making money, although I'm certain we could have squeezed them harder. They were only one of our businesses.

We drank the vodka, shot glass by shot glass, toasting our way through the bottles. "The business!" – the first toast. I suggested that. "To Ukraine!" – that was Zhenia. "To our women!" – I made the traditional third toast.

I picture his face as we made those toasts. His small, round head, his silky black hair, his six-thousand-dollar suit. His smooth face that could either look innocent as a child, or sneaky as a fox outside a hen-house. Of course, I preferred the sneaky look, but he managed to fool people with the innocent one. It made me a bit sick and a bit proud when he did it. He managed to persuade people that he was a good guy – that somehow he had just ended up in his position by a lot of luck and sweet-facing. Then they'd think he was a fool they could trick, and that's when he'd double-bluff them and take what he wanted. He'd done it so many times I sometimes felt like yawning when he started the routine. That's not my style. I'm more direct. I don't have the short, sneaky thing. I'm six-foot-four. I can't pull off sneaky. I just go in and I'm pretty straightforward about what I want and what's going to happen if I don't get it. When you've got six-foot-four of fist leaning over you, you're going to make a decision fast.

Zhenia had his innocent face on when we made the first toast. I raised my glass: "To business!" We clinked. We knocked them back. It was Nemiroff Gold. One of my favourites. So maybe he wasn't plotting against me, then?

We ate some *salo* and black bread. We ate some pickled cucumbers and cabbage with juniper berries. We ate some herring.

The second toast: "To Ukraine!" Zhenia made the toast. His face? Innocent again. That was always an ironic toast, as our country is rotten through and through, and that's why we're so rich. But we like to make it. We were watching some of the other tables from behind our curtains – we could see most of the restaurant. There was a traditional band playing: drums and double bass, accordion and violin. *Barvinochok*, that was the band. The restaurant was loud and there was some heavy drinking going on. There were some family groups, some business tables – a good mix. We had a big plate of fresh vegetables on the table. Peppers and tomatoes and cucumbers, radishes, bunches of dill, parsley and spring onion. I took a fresh cucumber and bit into it.

We didn't meet often enough anymore, Zhenia and I. We managed separate parts of the business-holding. On the factories side, I had the tyres and rubber. He had the bottled drinks and canned foods. On the financial side, I ran the bank and he ran the consulting firm. We ran the holding together. It had always been our agreement: steal together, share together, all equal. It couldn't have been more simple.

The third toast. I made it: "To our women!" The classic. And now I see his face. It was the sneaky face. I lifted my glass, we didn't quite clink – the glasses didn't touch, and I brought my glass towards my face, and it looked like he was grimacing, but no – it was his sneaky face. He knows! I'm sure of it! The bastard knows that I've taken Kotik from him. *Yo, moyo.* Why didn't I see it before? No wonder Kotik hasn't been answering the phone. He's paid her more. He's moved her to a new apartment. He's changed her phone number. Damn it. So, he knows about Kotik. I'm sure of that. But what about Katya? He couldn't know about Katya. If she told him, she'd be dead. And if he found out, I'd be dead. If he found out he would rip my heart out of my body. And that would start with cutting off my lifeblood. That's what he would do. He would cut me out of the business. He would strip everything away from me. He would twist all the parts that hurt the most. This is worse than I thought. Katya!

Breathe.

Breakfast time.

The monk came to me again. He checked my arm where it was bleeding. He sat with me. He looked into my eyes and I couldn't help it. I started crying again. I was thinking of Katya, lovely Katya. My Katerina. I am so worried for her. *Katya, I ask myself for the thousandth time, Katya, why did you have to marry Zhenia? Why did you choose him? Why did you not marry me?* At school, Katya was so breathtakingly beautiful that all the teachers were in love with her, as well as all the pupils. She has one eye blue and one eye green. She has so much blonde hair you could make a hay bale out of it. She is tall and her legs are so shapely they make you feel like weeping from lust. You feel like you can't physically survive around her beauty. And she chose Zhenia! Short, sneaky, round-headed little Zhenia. My best friend. I thought I would die when they started dating. I thought he was lying to me. And then I saw them together.

"Why?" I asked her. "I would do anything for you! I would lay down in the road and let a tank run over me. Why him?"

"He's going to be a millionaire, Vanechka," she replied.

"You? I don't know. Maybe. But Zhenia, he's going to give me the life I need."

A practical girl. Nothing wrong with that. And it was only after she'd given Zhenia two children that she even let me touch her. Oh god, the first time I touched her. And the thought that Zhenia had had her all that time. I felt so sick with envy. It made me want her so badly it was all I could think about. I'd think about her when Eva was giving me pleasure. I'd even think about her when I was with Kotik, although I knew that was crazy, because Kotik can hold her own with anyone. And, of course, Zhenia knew that. He knew how crazy I was about her. But he won her. And then I had to shut up and not talk about her.

It took me twelve years to get into her knickers.

And now I've lost everything.

Breathe.

Francis

Four-thirty a.m.

Nine-thirty at night in London.

I am not at home frying a steak and sautéing beans while Jimme is stretched out on the sofa, reading the news on his phone.

I am sitting in an enormous hall in the middle of Thailand surrounded by men with rings on their toes and tie-dye T-shirts, coughing, sneezing and shuffling. I am meant to be observing the triangle of sensation below my nose. Not my breath any more. Today I observe my left nostril, my right nostril and the line of upper lip where the breath meets skin. *Alors.* I can do this. But I am not doing this. I am thinking about Jimme.

We met in a gay bar in London. He was breath-catchingly attractive and seemed to be welcoming everyone who spoke to him as a long-lost brother, a generous and joyful smile on his face. Medium height, dressed in designer blue jeans and a black T-shirt, he could have been in any capital in the world – a nightclub in Milan, a café in Paris, a martini bar in Montreal.

It was a small, sophisticated place that I had found early on. It wasn't exactly that I was looking for men. There had just been so many women in Paris and it felt like something different would suit my move to London.

"I am François," I said, taking the bar stool beside him.

"Jimme," he replied, and he held out his hand and shook mine with such warmth, physical and ethereal, that I felt accepted and embraced. It was a circle of generosity that was vastly welcoming to someone moving to a new city.

"What do you do, Jimme?" I asked him.

"I am a maths teacher," he said. "And an electrician. I am seeking asylum, you see, in this country."

"Where are you seeking asylum from, Jimme?" For some reason, I couldn't stop saying his name.

"From my country of Uganda," he answered me, with a huge smile. "A beautiful country, the very best country. But they are not very happy about some aspects of my life, you see."

I nodded. "I've heard. How long have you been here, Jimme?" His name again.

"Three years," he replied. "I am asking for asylum for three years, but it is very slow. This is why I am now an electrician. I have to do something, you know. It is not very legal, but three years is a long time."

"Where do you live?" I asked. I couldn't help myself. I think I was already in love at that point. From the moment when he had shaken my hand and shown me what warmth he had in his soul. I wanted that warmth.

"I live near here." He leaned forward to whisper in my ear. "It isn't very nice at my place. Maybe yours will be better? Unless your wife is there?"

The tingling in my ear made me shiver.

"I've got drinks at my flat," I said. "Will you come?"

After a month, I persuaded Jimme to move in with me. His warmth was always there, in the morning, getting ready for work, in the evening, after a day modelling attack-scenarios at Hartbridge. I knew his warmth was not something I would be able to own, but I was grateful for sharing it, for each day I was within its circle.

Jimme was the most laidback person I had ever met. I mean,

laidback yet also productive. He had trained and worked as a maths teacher in Uganda and had escaped when it was discovered he was having a relationship with a man. He would have to requalify as a teacher in order to work in London, which he couldn't do until he had been granted asylum. His father had been an electrician, and Jimme could fix most things, so he helped people out on the quiet, taking pocket change for the work. He was grateful for the small amount of money he had and the gifts he received from friends. He was grateful to be in the country. He seemed happy to be with me. But all the happiness and the warmth and the gratitude was so much a part of who he was that I couldn't take it personally. He would have been the same joyful man in another situation. It was not a result of anything I had done, it was something I was lucky to be in proximity to. It wasn't my cooking, or buying him clothes, or us walking on a Saturday morning around the neighbourhood; all those things were opportunities that had been created by him and his generous character.

Of course, I worried about all of that. Even when I was at my happiest and in the most caring relationship, I worried because I did not possess it. It could disappear as quickly as it had appeared. I knew I should appreciate it even more for that reason. But I am human. I wanted to feel safe.

"Marry me," I asked Jimme one morning. It was a Sunday and we were pulling on hiking boots ready to climb Black Down, the moody hill outside Haslemere where Tennyson used to stride, caped and with a soul full of inspiration, a hundred years past. "It will sort out all your asylum problems. We'll get a bigger flat. You'll be able to retrain here and work as a maths teacher again."

Jimme was beside me on the sofa, a dark red velvet piece with large buttons holding down the material. He leaned over and took my face in his hands. He kissed me. "François, I cannot marry you," he said. "I cannot bring this shame on my family."

"But they know who you are," I argued. "They know why you are living in London. Do they know about me?"

"Yes, yes, they know about you."

"Then there is nothing to hide. Marry me! Everything will work out."

"It is very easy for you," he replied. "But family is close in Uganda. There is no marriage there between men. People would see it as something very bad. It would bring disgrace on my family. My sisters would not find husbands."

"But if you do it, and show them that it is a natural thing, then you can help to change their minds."

"I don't want to change anyone's mind," Jimme answered. His face grew sad. "I love you, François. But one day, I will marry a woman. I have agreed it with my mother. She will find one in Uganda and we will marry here. There will be no shame on my family."

I knew that it had not been an illusion: the affair, the passion, the walking hand-in-hand. Somehow, Jimme was able to give all of himself to me, and still keep his true self hidden away, unreachable by anyone. It was not something I was able to do: I threw myself and my heart into the hands of each lover, open to easy breakage at any point. I do not know how Jimme had learned to do this. It was an admirable quality. He was loved by everyone and yet still safe in his heart. He loved openly, but not with vulnerability. He lived on the whim of a country but felt more secure in his life than me.

"Jimme, I don't think it has to be like that." I was really hurting by then. I reached for his hand and held it, our hands the same size, both of us with slender fingers, dry in the autumn cool, mine yellow with tufts of black hair, his deep brown, smooth, with no hair, and pink around the nails.

He didn't answer, so I asked: "When do you think your marriage will happen? How long do we have together?"

Once again he didn't reply, but leaned towards me and we

kissed, and in the kiss was all the beauty of temporality. In that kiss was everything I should have understood about Jimme, but was too stupid to learn. That we possess nothing. That everything passes. That the beauty of the moment is all there is. That now is the living divine.

I learned nothing.

Nothing at all.

"Will you be here when I get back?"

Jimme was making coffee in the espresso machine I had brought over from Paris. He made two for himself and two for me and brought the cups over to the sofa. The flat seemed to be covered in newspapers and the sun was shining on the surfaces, lighting the dust on the velvet sofa, on the edges of cushions, on the covers of magazines.

"If you want to move out while I'm gone that's fine," I said. "I just mean that I want you to do what you want."

He still didn't reply. He sat holding his coffee, his back straight.

"I love you, Jimme," I said. The coffee was steaming and the smell was like his kiss: perfect in that dusty sunshine, in that moment, he and I sitting in that apartment. "But I want you to be happy."

I couldn't say any more. Ten days of silence in Thailand. Jimme would have time to re-evaluate everything, to make new choices, to move on. I could come back and he might be married to a woman. Yes, I suppose that was my greatest fear. Or that he would simply be gone. But I was ready for that. I would accept that and I wanted him to know.

We sipped our coffee. He didn't answer any of my questions. The words remained in the room, lit by the sunlight, the dust glittering on the surfaces, the coffee steam illuminated, its smell so powerful.

I find it painful not to know if Jimme is on that sofa now, stretched out, his long arms, always in a T-shirt, dark on the red velvet, his hair short, alive like fresh heather, his face ready to look up in joy, to welcome me with happiness, to disappear forever.

DAY FOUR

Laeticia

I FEEL the gaze of two men in the room. Their eyes have been following me. They are both sitting on the edge of the men's section, right up against the white line.

The tall one is trying not to fidget. He has enormous tension in his body. He is holding it still as if he is about to go into a boxing ring. The other one is calmer, but he has a sadness to him. I know they can see me. I feel them watching me. I imagine they are letting their minds wander. There aren't many participants here who aren't from Thailand so I suppose I stand out. They're probably stripping me naked in their heads right now.

Well, let's play along. Let's take a trip into male fantasy land. Let's see if I can break this dream palace that men can enter and where, in their fantasies, which are legitimised by all the pornography available to them everywhere, they can do anything they desire to women... these pillars of flesh who only exist for their sexual fulfilment.

I will break this.

Here we go.

Breathe.

I imagine it's late at night and I can't sleep so I've taken a walk around the compound next to the jungle, but I've taken a wrong turn and I've strayed onto the men's path. It's hot, so all I'm wearing is a flimsy nightgown. It's a black lace number from the Victoria's Secret selection in my bag. I've forgotten to wear any panties and my cleavage is spilling out of the frilly top.

That's about right, isn't it? That's the kind of thing men are conditioned to fantasise about? Let's continue.

I'm leaning over a wooden handrail, gazing out at the jungle with a dreamy look in my eyes.

"Ahem."

Somehow, I hadn't caught sight of the two men smoking a forbidden cigarette nearby.

"It's late," one says.

"You must be a little cold," the other says. They both take a step towards me.

"Actually, I'm burning up," I say, in my huskiest voice. "I just need to get this thing off me." I start to tug at the flimsy material barely covering my body.

"We can help you," says the first one.

"You're right, it's far too hot tonight. It's the jungle heat," says the second one, and he slips off the unbuttoned shirt he was wearing and is just in a pair of loose shorts. His erection is pushing against the front.

The first one has come up to me. He's in a T-shirt and boxer shorts. He flicks the cigarette away.

"Let's get you out of that nightdress," he says.

He leans in and his hands drift over the see-through material. The aftershave he is wearing is sharp, expensive and invigorating. It is the same aftershave worn by the man who raped me. My body twitches to that smell. I look towards the face of the second man and it is Juan. He is staring at me with those brown eyes that know my body and could touch me in places that made me cling to him and hide my face against his shoulder as he carried me through the clouds, flying, flying for those moments, flying and clinging and hiding and he would hold me as I shuddered around him and then we would fly together, not hiding but open, loud, laughing delight. Juan Juan Juan. Yes, somehow it is his face that is now flicking a second cigarette away.

My body is ready.

Two men, two towering erections.

The hand of the first man is circling my waist, lifting the nightdress. I take his fingers in my hand and raise them to my mouth. I draw two of them in and suck. He has begun to stroke me lower and lower. I am ready. I breathe in his aftershave. I remember how my body did not fight back in the Paris courtyard. The ancient stones. The clicking heels. His trousers unzipped. I bite down on the fingers.

I take up my machine gun and I fire it at the men in my hut. Blood spatters out of their bodies. They are screaming. I point it at each of them and let the bullets roar and clatter. They are delving and piercing into the flesh and the muscle and the bone. They are causing extraordinary pain. They are causing mutilation and death. My finger is jammed on the hot trigger. It's burning my finger. My entire body is wildly aroused. I love this burning. It is my clitoris burning. I'm going to orgasm right here. I pull my finger harder back and the bullets pierce and screech into these motherfuckers. And my daughters! I run out of my hut, through the dead bodies, and my daughters are being dragged away by more men. *"Meninas!"* I call out. "Girls!" And I toss them machine guns. They catch them easily and, with practised movements, they open fire on their would-be-captors. The men are soon dead, yet they keep on firing. Let their bodies be a warning to anyone who touches a woman.

"Nice going, my girls!" I call out. "Let's hunt down the others, shall we?"

My daughters sling the machine guns over their shoulders and pull on their jungle boots. All the aggressors should have been mown down by now because, suddenly, all women everywhere, all over the world, are able to defend themselves. If anyone comes near them, they are gunned down by well-practised machine gun fire, and left out to rot as an example. In the law courts, the default is to side with the women, unless there is extraordinary evidence that shows the death was unprovoked. And, really, define "unprovoked." Aren't the men just asking for it? Of course, it helps that all the judges and lawyers are women, and the entire government too, and the police force. And that they all carry massive guns. Men have to cover their sorry heads with blankets or even their entire bodies with giant sheets so we don't have to see their erect penises bulging out of their rapist trousers.

I digress.

I'm biting the fingers of the first man.

"Fuck!" he screams. "What are you doing?" He's screaming it in a foreign accent. Polish? Italian?

He pulls his arm away. I grasp the hand that was stroking my body and pull it hard up behind him. "Think it's your right to take whatever you want?" I ask him.

"Fuck! Fuck! No!" he screams.

"I can't understand you," I say. "You mean, 'No, you don't like what I'm doing,' or 'No, it is not your right?'"

"It's not my right!" he bellows. At least he understands this much English.

"Good." I wrench his arm upwards so that it breaks. He screams. I let him go.

I turn to Juan.

"You think you can win my trust and build dreams with my future and know my deepest confidences, and then throw them on the garbage heap like a pile of crap?" I ask.

Juan is doing the dreamy eyes at me. He figures he can still swing this situation over to his side. He remembers so many of my sensitivities, he estimates there is a chance.

I resist his eyes. Those eyes!

"It was a question," I say. "Don't make me bring out the machine gun."

He flinches, but perseveres. "Everything we had was real, beautiful Laeticia," he says. "It is my weakness that is also real. I am flawed. I kneel before you."

He tries to kneel but I shake my head.

"Not working," I say.

There is a huge pile of rubbish just beyond the path. I can see faeces, fish heads, mouldy food.

"This is where you emptied out my trust and dreams and my love for you and my confidences," I say. "This is the value you attached to them. This is the value they had to you. Therefore, this is where you belong."

I have to do it quickly. I know he is strong. But I am a black belt in self-defence and karate. I plan the move in my head before I carry it out, then – one, two – I kick his legs out, catch his weight and throw him. He lands sideways on the rubbish heap, his face neatly buried in a pile of excrement.

"There we go," I say. "And, by the way, I have a daughter and you are the biological father. She's never going to know anything about you."

The rapist is holding his arm and crying. "Get over there," I say and point to the rubbish heap. He limps over and sits on it, next to Juan.

I pull off the Victoria's Secret nightdress and throw it on the pile. I am naked.

"This is my body," I say. "It's not a fucking consumer product. It belongs to me. I'll do with it what I please. The only way you get near it is by filling out the paperwork."

One more thing. "If you think about passing judgement on it," I warn, "that'll be another broken arm."

Just for good measure I take all the pornography magazines in the world and put them on the rubbish pile. Then I set the pile alight. Juan and the rapist get up from the burning heap and flee into the jungle.

It's alright.

My daughters are waiting there with guns.

Ivan

I dreamed about Katya last night.

I dreamed about the orange monk.

When I awoke to the gong at four a.m., I wondered if either of them was real.

My face in the mirror is looking better. I'm sleeping so deeply it's like I'm knocked unconscious every night.

Sitting here for hours in the room, my bites itching, the squawking parrots and the jungle outside, the videos they show us – I feel it's all calming me. It's showing me what deep stress I've been living under for so long. Business stress, home stress, Katya stress, the stress of betraying Zhenia with her. Even when we went on holiday to the Seychelles together, it was the same stress, just on a beach. Even when I took Kotik to Paris and we stayed at the Georges V, I was still on my phone for ninety percent of the trip.

But here: silence. I haven't said a word for three days. Just resting from the sound of my own voice. And no phone. No desperate e-mails. No people to threaten. No business decisions. No Eva asking for money. No Kotik needing a bank transfer. Not even Katya. I don't remember when I was last more than one metre away from my phone. In the sauna, my bodyguard has the phone in one pocket and a gun in the other. In the shower, I keep it in the bathroom in case Eva starts looking through it.

And here? It's locked in the safe in the administrator's office with all the other phones. Anyone could just walk in and smash the door and take it. But I don't care. There's nothing to find there. I don't control the businesses anymore. Zhenia has probably sold them off by now. All he needed was to establish the majority stake in the holding company, and then he could do what he wanted. Fifty-one percent. The number of control. He took it.

"Fifty thousand dollars," Katya told me. "For every time we meet."

We were in the Buddha Bar. Zhenia was out of town. Her body hadn't changed an inch since she'd had Zhenia's two children. I can't imagine how expensive that must have been. I know she flew straight to an Italian spa the moment the second one was born. Sitting opposite me, her hair was down to her waist, and there were the eyes, one blue, one green.

"Really?" I asked. I'm not a stupid man, but those eyes were sucking out my brains.

"You must transfer it to my account before the meeting," she said. "It is non-negotiable."

She opened her Chanel handbag and took out a piece of paper. "Here are the bank details," she said. "I will require an initial deposit of one hundred thousand dollars. That is non-refundable. That is to show me you are serious."

"I'm serious, Katya!"

"And then afterwards, as I have told you, it is fifty thousand dollars in advance of every meeting."

Damn, she was smart. It was the right price. I couldn't buy her an apartment or a car, like other mistresses would get.

Zhenia had given her all of those, although they were in his name, I was sure of that. I knew what she was doing. She was buying her independence.

And how much did I pay her in total? The first hundred. Then we must have met twenty times. That's a million bucks I paid her. She's got an account with a million dollars sitting in it. Smart girl. It's still pin money, though. She can't escape to America with a million dollars. It's not enough to start a new life, unless she has a rich man waiting on the other side.

The monk is at breakfast again. I think he's adopted me. He checks my wounds and nods and then he looks into my eyes. I glance at his face – it is the first time I'm not crying so I can see what he looks like. It is smooth, as if he's just had a hundred thousand dollars of plastic surgery. He must be forty or fifty but his skin is like a slice of mango. It's like an avocado.

Anyway, he does the praying-bowing thing and I do the praying-bowing thing back. It feels odd that there is no kind of transaction between us. He doesn't need anything from me. I don't owe him anything. There isn't a question of trust or distrust. It stirs something in me. This monk is relating to me like no one in my life has before. Just like a human being and nothing more.

In fact, I can run through the list of people in my life and what they wanted from me.

Father: nothing, he left before I was born.

Mother, from age zero to twenty: good behaviour, silence, homework, silence, wood carried, silence, success in business. Age twenty onwards: a lot of money, regular visits, grandchildren, me slagging off Eva, me eating her food every time she cooked it, me supporting her when she slagged off Eva and Eva's food.

Eva: money, marriage, money, children, money.

Zhenia: partnership, brotherhood, co-thievery.

Children: toys, clothes, money.

Kotik: money.

Katya: money.

There.

And this monk is just looking in my eyes. He wants to see *me*. To see who I am. To see what my heart says. To see why I am hurting.

I think I love him.

What would my monk tell me to do, if we could speak?

I'd tell him: "My best friend in the world has betrayed me. He has taken away my business. I have no more money. I have no friend. My wife will leave me."

My monk would look at me with those clear vodka eyes and avocado face.

"It was my fault," I'd tell him eventually. "I'd been sleeping with his wife for the past year. I think he found out. You see, I'd always been in love with her. She's got one green eye and one blue one," I'd explain.

We'd take a breath, my monk and I. This breathing is good for us. We know that when we inhale, we breathe in all the good things and when we exhale, we let go of all the stress and bad thoughts. I've heard that enough times.

So, we take a breath.

"It's all my fault," I go on. "I was sleeping with his wife, and paying her too. And I was sleeping with his mistress. I was also siphoning money off some of our businesses. I didn't even need the money. We both had enough money. I just wanted to see if I could do it. A kind of personal test. I guess he found that out, too."

The monk's avocado face is looking at me. He is entirely

calm. He is not judging me. He is accepting me as the traitorous, greedy, conniving, possessive, domineering, bullying, threatening, aggressive, yet sometimes generous man that I am.

He sees all of me! He accepts me! He loves me!

I love him too! Oh, how I love him too.

Nobody has ever looked into my rotten, greedy soul and just nodded. Just said, "Yes, you are you. It's okay. I'm me and you are you. I love you, brother."

It's such a beautiful thing that I want to cry again. For the first time in my life, I've been accepted. By an avocado-faced man wearing an orange sheet. But I don't care. He's a beautiful man. He's a holy man. He's my brother.

There. Now I'm crying.

Try not to sniff too loudly.

The people to my left and right are glancing round. It doesn't help being six-foot-four. When you cry, people notice.

There goes another Adidas suit.

Let the tears come.

Zhenia took everything from me. Zhenia, who has been my brother since that first day in kindergarten. He pulled my ear. I punched him in the stomach. I never had to hide from him.

But only my monk sees the good behind who I am. Zhenia saw me and then took revenge on me. My monk would never punish me. He would love me. Zhenia, you didn't love me well enough. You knew me, but you had to come after me. You knew what a traitorous bastard I was. You knew I always wanted Katya. Why did you have to come and punish me like that? We could have talked it out! We could have come to an arrangement!

Breathe.

Observe the breath.

Breathe.

What would my monk say?

He would say: "Brother, ask him for forgiveness."

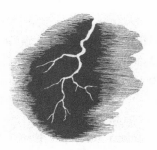

Francis

Four-thirty a.m.

Nine-thirty at night in London.

I am not pacing the streets of Brixton crying as I picture threats to the world in every cloud, crowd, container around me. I am not lying in a ditch in Shepperton waiting to be exterminated by a Heat Ray.

I am sitting cross-legged on a small blue cushion. I am in the middle of the Thai jungle. I am surrounded by people who seek peace.

I am, for the third day, observing my nose.

What I have understood about my nose, after ten hours of observation, which is, needless to say, longer than I have ever spent observing my nose: it is not, as I previously imagined, one unified entity. My nose has two chambers that appear to work separately from each other. Let me take the shape. Each nostril chamber is quite different from the other. The left chamber is narrow, lopsided and slightly misshapen. The right chamber is wider, of a more regular shape, rounder at the base. I observe the breath being pushed from the chambers onto my upper lip – a sensation I have never been aware of before. But in the silence and in the length of the minutes here, I can spend breath after breath experiencing the tickles of carbon dioxide upon the hairs of my top lip and the draw of oxygen through the cilia-hung caverns of my nostrils.

A great discovery: the system of breathing changes

approximately every hour. For one hour, the left nostril draws and expels the breath and the right nostril is entirely blocked. By what, and how, I cannot imagine. The following hour, the left nostril is entirely blocked and the right is dominant, with the breath working only through this channel. And then: switch.

I am entranced. I am fascinated. Has this been happening for every breath I have taken since my birth? What other secrets does my body hold that I could learn through simple observation? I would find out, but for these morning hours we are forbidden to move beyond the nose. This afternoon, we will be permitted to transfer our attention outwards, to the great swathes of human flesh that lie beyond the nostrils. We will be taught the ancient Vipassana technique that led the Buddha to enlightenment. Ah, the anticipation! What will be revealed? What systems, with their own logic, will be discovered? Systems that have been functioning for all of my physical existence on this planet and yet I have been blind to. As I have read a thousand books and written thousands of words on the secrets of the physical world – double first in natural sciences, as Hilary smugly predicted – I have neglected to discover the most basic functions of my own body.

Jimme did not react well to my increasing sense of panic. He had an innately positive view of the world, and saw general peace and happiness around him and good outcomes everywhere. He didn't even hold a grudge against the people who would have killed him after his relationship with a man was discovered.

"It is the tradition of my country," he said to me. "How can a country remain what it is, if it destroys all the traditions?"

"So, if there was a vote on legalising homosexuality in Uganda, would you vote against it?"

We were in a bar around the corner from my flat. Jimme was

drinking a gin and tonic. I had a glass of red wine. As always, he was drawing attention from both women and men. His face, deepest brown, intensely peaceful; his smile made of the happiness we all seek.

He smiled now. "I would vote against it, François," he said. "I don't want my country to be full of gays. It isn't how it should be."

I was already growing used to his positions, and I didn't feel anger now at his words, but perhaps a sadness.

I sought his eyes. "Jimme," I said. "Traditions have to evolve. Where could you find more tradition than in my countries: England and France? But I can live freely here as a gay man or a straight man and I can still love and respect the traditions. There have always been gay men and straight men in these countries. But now, we can be a part of society and share the traditions. We can share the cultural history of the country, which is something that is always evolving."

I took a sip of wine.

"Even the traditions you are talking about," I went on, glancing at his face to check he was still with me. He was, his head tilted, his face open and interested. "Even those traditions that you respect and want to preserve, they came from other traditions. They weren't the very first traditions in your country ever to be developed. It's how a nation works. You keep some, you adjust some, you preserve some. You move on, and everyone is happier and richer and better educated."

I decided I was sounding preachy, so I stopped.

"Jimme?"

He sipped his gin and tonic as if we had been talking about which film to see, then he reached out and put his hand on my shoulder. He looked earnestly into my eyes. I gazed back at his, which I was always trying to catch the colour of, the sparks of orange and brown in circles of almost-black. His eyes were so calm and happy that I immediately felt like an inferior person, like someone who knew less about the world, someone who was running around in their Western capitalist-fuelled need-fulfilment, while Jimme just existed and lived, and took and gave pleasure. He possessed a calm that I would never know.

"François, you have never been to Uganda. It is different. You have your system here, in your France and your England. And we have our system there. It is not your system to change."

He kept his hand on my shoulder a few moments more, and I felt the conviction of his words, and the physical body behind that conviction, willing to change itself, subjugate itself, to that conviction. It reminded me, just for an instant, of the choices of saints in the history of Christianity. Of the people who made decisions that their bodies would have to follow, and how that gave such power to their purpose. There was, without a doubt, something of the saint in Jimme. Something of the innocent. And yet, I could not agree.

"I've been to Africa, Jimme," I said. "I've been to Morocco. I've been to Cape Town."

He laughed, and we let it go. We ordered more drinks and I told him about the teacher-training courses I had found for him. He was happy and grateful. We drank and, for him, nothing had changed.

What a gift, to be so imperturbable. Not to live in duality, as I do, in anticipation, as I do, in terror, as I do. What a gift, to take the world as a delight.

"If an alien civilisation were to develop a way to manipulate the amount of gravity on Earth, then we could be rendered inactive in a short period of time."

Leila Massey. Writer of science fiction and our instructor for a two-week course at our secret London location.

She continued.

"If gravity was halved from the current 9.8 metres per

second squared to 4.9, the human population would gradually fall ill and die, as the atmospheric oxygen would no longer be held close to the surface of the earth and no one without an oxygen suit would be able to breathe.

"Going in the other direction, if gravity were increased by just five percent to 10.3 metres per second squared, then the earth would be pulled into a tighter elliptical orbit, causing our seasons to become more extreme, together with weather changes drastic enough to spark worldwide famine and crash the global economy. Now this could be done as a prelude to a full-scale invasion, or simply to rid the planet of unwanted inhabitants prior to re-habitation by a new species."

Leila Massey paused and looked around the room, examining the surprised faces in the audience. Then she raised her voice for the climax.

"Destruction of the human race and colonisation of the planet don't have to come through alien arrival or a direct attack. We have to make the assumption that any alien civilisation advanced enough to be in a position of colonisation would bring techniques that are highly developed, highly efficient and possibly proven on other planets."

Our first session of learning to look into the future and think outside known facts.

Nobody came out smiling.

DAY FIVE

Laeticia

"ANABEL, I need to tell you something."

I'd finally got her on a video call. She was busy all the time these days, just like me when I was in New York. But I'd got through to her. She was scanning my eyes for the news. Her hair was in an afro, the edges of it somewhere off the frame of the screen.

"It's Juan," she said. "He's done something dumb."

"It's worse," I said. I tried not to cry. Because it was Juan as well, but I couldn't even say that right now.

"Shit," she said. "Tell me."

"I was raped."

"Oh my god," she said. Her hand went up to her mouth.

"Laeticia, oh my god," she said again. "I'm so sorry. When did it happen?"

"Two weeks ago."

"Does Juan know?"

This was the hard one to answer. I held up my hand to her, asking for a moment. I took a breath.

"He's gone." I dug my fingernails into my leg. "He was cheating." I pushed them in so that I could feel the pain deep in my skin. "I'm pregnant," I said.

Breathe.

"To us!"

On graduation, we had both won jobs at the United Nations. I was joining the UNHCR to work on refugee issues, and she was on the speech-writing team for the Secretary General. She would be in the main building on the East River, while I was just across the road, with the rush of First Avenue flowing below me.

"To us! Watch out world!"

Back from another party weekend in Rio, our stellar degrees in the bag and job offers accepted, we were in our favourite cocktail bar in New York: Bar SixtyFive at the Rainbow Room. We had martinis, mine vodka and hers gin, and below us was spread out the entire island of Manhattan, a smorgasbord of ambition and money, power and brains. It was ours for the taking.

We drank, and watched the dark red sun light up the island, then fade to the twinkle of dusk as the lights of the buildings grew into sharper focus, the natural light seamlessly replaced by the glow of the skyscrapers and the illuminated avenues.

"Here is to nothing ever stopping us." Anabel raised the next cocktail high. Her hair was a chaos of dark red curls. She had a plan for the next twenty years. The United Nations, then working for a congresswoman, then for the department of state, then becoming Secretary of State. My plan? A few years at the United Nations, then perhaps returning to Brazil to join the civil service and get in line to be an ambassador; or join a political think-tank; or become an Americas trade consultant. My path was less clear than Anabel's, but I relied more on intuition to take me round each bend.

"Nothing ever stopping us!" I clinked my glass to hers and the vodka slipped down my throat, with the faint tang of olive.

We were single. We were powerful. We were women.

Breathe.

After the rape, I lay on the floor in the corridor and shook. I tried to curl up into a ball but I couldn't, my limbs were shaking so hard. They had failed me; they had not run away; my arms had not punched; my fingers had not poked out his eyes; my body had struggled in the most minimal way. The mass of his chest and arms had trapped me in that courtyard opening. At the end, when he was finished, he fastened his trousers, keeping me enclosed there. He leaned forward and whispered, *"C'est ça que tu voulais, ma belle. Je l'ai su dès que je t'ai vue."* This is what you wanted, my beautiful. I knew it the moment I saw you.

I lay shaking and then I managed to lever myself onto my hands and knees and crawled through my flat into the kitchen. There was a bottle of cognac – Juan's, it was the strongest drink in the apartment. I took a glass, staggered to the bed and poured it. Deep red brown. A beautiful colour. Grande Champagne. One of Juan's extravagant purchases. I sipped.

C'est ça que tu voulais, ma belle. My arms calmed. I could hold the glass. I sipped. *C'est ça que tu voulais.* My legs were still. I pulled them up to my chin. I started to be aware of my body. I could feel wetness inside. I sipped. *I'm sorry, my child. If you're going to live, I'm sorry. I need to drink this. I'm sorry if it gives you brain damage. I'm sorry. I'm sorry.*

I had a small stomach, more like a bloating than a pregnancy swell. I could not look down at it. My knees were jammed under my chin. I sipped. *I must drink. I must wash. I must breathe. I must visit the doctor.*

I thought about the police. I could have gone right then. I could have filed a report for rape. I could have had him found and put on trial. I would be examined. I would be asked for detail after detail. I would repeat his look, his smell, his touch. I thought about Juan, somewhere right then, with a woman who was not me. I thought of my café, and the staff waiting outside at nine a.m. I thought about the child inside me. *C'est ça que tu voulais.*

No. I did not have the strength. If I could have taken time from work and had someone by my side to hold me – then yes. But the man I thought was my life partner was a burning scarecrow. My café was as tenuous as the latest business fad. It rested entirely upon me and my energy to propel it to success. If I let one more thing pull me down, then everything would come crashing to the ground. No police. No report. No questions. No investigation.

Sip. Thread of red brown fire. Hot water ahead. Push down the rage. Calm the shaking limbs. There would be a time for rage. There would be a time for revenge. There would be a time to raise up the fury and light it for the world to see.

But not that night.

That night would be a rush of hot water and soap. That night I would wash and wash and wash, my face, my hair, my trunk, my insides, my traitorous legs, my cowardly arms. My clothes I would roll into a bag, ready to destroy. I would step out of the shower and scrub myself with a rough towel until my skin was glowing red, my cells upstanding and new. Tomorrow, I would cut my hair at lunchtime. *Something fresh,* I would say to the coiffeur. *Different. Let's try short.*

By the next afternoon, the woman of yesterday would not exist. Not skin, nor hair, nor clothes.

Voila! I would twirl in the café for my staff to admire the new look. *Let's plan a new event! Now that the lunch rush is finished. Let us invite a speaker for an evening talk. I know a great professor in Brazil. Let's see if she will come.*

They would gather around me, my staff, infused with ideas and clean energy and excitement for our project, and my new hair *à la mode,* and the burning flush of my cheeks.

"It is alright," the doctor said. It was a woman. I told her everything. The rape. The cognac. Juan. The café. "It is alright." She scanned the baby.

"Et psychologiquement? L'enfant? Est-ce qu'il sera affecté?"

She pulled a wry face. "It is not my job to say that. Perhaps some effect will come from what you choose to tell her. It makes a difference, *non?"*

I nodded. It made a difference.

Ivan

I'm in trouble.

I pushed a monk.

They've sent me to my room.

It wasn't my fault. I went to breakfast as usual and took my bowl of *kasha* and raisins and brown sugar. All going well. I waited for my monk to arrive. And there was someone approaching in orange, and I imagine my stupid big hairy face lit up like a *yolka*, a New Year tree, covered in fairy lights, as he came towards me, and – it was a different monk! They were trying to fool me with a different monk. I felt so stupid and betrayed. I thought: *They are laughing at you. They are making an idiot of you. They think you won't notice if they switch the monks.*

I got so angry and I was shaking my head and pointing at him and then he was doing the praying-bowing thing that my monk does and I didn't know how to show him I didn't want him, so I pushed him. Quite hard. He fell over, anyway. I guess that showed him that I didn't want him. Then a lot of people came running over and they got the monk away and then a couple of them motioned for me to follow, and they took me back to my room.

I've been here ever since.

Did they really think I wouldn't notice if they swapped monks?

I want my monk back.

It's different being here on my own. Everyone is meditating in the big white hall. Women, men, monks. Here I am alone.

Is this what prison is like? I never sat inside, but I know plenty who did. Quite a few of us from school ended up behind bars. Some of them worked for me afterwards. They were rough after jail. Tattoos and curse-laden speech. There was a line that they had crossed, something in their eyes and something physical – the way they stood. You couldn't bring them to a nice restaurant. Or maybe it was the leather jackets.

In the nineties, it was just a free-for-all. Everything was for sale. Everything was for stealing. Life was worth nothing. All the pensions had gone and factories were closing everywhere. The only reliable thing was your grandmother's house – if the property had been granted to her – and the cucumbers she grew in the garden. Nothing else was fixed.

So, everyone was selling. Run-down bottle factory? Give me ten thousand dollars. Coal mine? Half a million. Four rubber plants? Twenty. People just wanted the cash. Then someone else would cut your fingers off until you signed ownership over to them for the price of the three fingers remaining on your left hand. Then someone would shoot him in the head while his girlfriend was sucking him off and the documents were theirs. All the while, the workers were turning up without being paid, month after month. Until they stopped working. Everything ground to a halt. Even if you owned the factory, you didn't have money to repair it or pay anyone. It had been sending false production reports to Moscow for the last ten years and was inefficient and none of the machinery worked. It was a pile of creaking bones.

But Zhenia and I were in our element. We were fighters. We got our hands on properties, then sold them for better ones. We stayed away from the finger-cutters and broke just enough of our own to put together a portfolio. Then we started the bank and began raking in money. Zhenia had Katya hidden away all this time. She was pregnant and he was pouring cash into some secret location where she could live in luxury while he fought in the trenches. It was a smart move.

And me? I had no one. I had Zhenia. I had my mother, planting cucumbers. There were women, plenty of women making quick money, trying to stay afloat. But none of them were Katya. So, I was alone.

Maybe that's what it's always been. All six-foot-four-inches of me. Alone. Perhaps that's what I have come here to realise: that I have always been alone. That I will always be alone. Two arms covered in black hair. Two legs. A grizzled head. A dick that's only truly wanted one woman.

Vision: I live in Thailand and have renounced the material life to become a monk. We are meditating in the great hall as we usually do at four a.m. There are twenty of us. I tower over them by two feet. My skin is a smooth nectarine. I haven't drunk vodka for six months. My liver thinks it has died and gone to heaven. It's on holiday. It's on the beach in the Seychelles. I'm wearing a huge orange sheet and nothing else. My cock is loose and comfortable. I haven't had a woman for six months but I find that brotherly love gives me more satisfaction nowadays. We meditate and the love starts flowing between us. It lifts us up. We have nothing, we monks; we own nothing. We have nothing to give or take, apart from good deeds and positive energy. It is a simple life. We are happy.

At breakfast we eat mangoes and porridge. The cook-monks have made it. After breakfast the cleaning-monks clean it all up.

Me? I am the strong monk. The river is blocked and so I pick up the boulders and clear it. The gate is broken so I lift the gate and it is fixed. The fruit-collecting-monks pick baskets of mangoes and I carry them back to our living quarters.

While I am carrying the mangoes, one of the brother-monks says: "Ukrainian-brother, it will be better if you carry the mangoes on your shoulders, not hanging from your arms. It is more efficient."

I hear the words. I have been taught that we should observe our reactions before we choose to step onto the path of action. So, I observe: heart pounding with anger, sending heat vibrations through my chest area; head dizzy with shame and self-doubt caused by the criticism; anger rising, rising, filling my head with heat that flows upwards to the top of my scalp and is trapped in a nest of hair; repeat of the rising anger, the dizziness fades, the anger intensifies and then eventually cools. My heart calms, the heat passes out of my scalp-hair-nest, the sensations fade. I am calm. I have observed the reaction.

Now, I make my choice. The old me would have turned round and swung the mango basket into his head and then kicked him to the dust. I am a monk, though. I choose my next step with a calm mind and a heart full of compassion. "Thank you, Thai-brother," I reply. "I will try that."

I lift the mango basket and, as I do so, I swing it round and slam it into his head.

Someone had to teach him a lesson. May as well be me, Ukrainian-monk-brother.

This is what it means to be rich.

Grandmother One dies. I am a poor man. I have dropped out of school and am indulging in some petty crime. My mother has no money and we eat soup made from the vegetables in the garden and pickles from the stacks of jars in the hallway. We have meat and cottage cheese if we trade our pickles for them. I have one set of clothes and I wear them all the time. If I want a drink of water, I pump it from the well in a bucket.

The funeral is simple. My mother is there, Zhenia, Zhenia's mother, Zhenia's grandmother and me. Zhenia's grandmother looks angry, but I know she is upset. She used to exchange barbed comments with my now-dead grandmother when they dropped us off at kindergarten, and it meant a lot to them both.

They lower the coffin into the grave and we have a gravestone with Grandmother's face carved on it from a photograph of her, aged around fifty. It's a terrible likeness but we can't afford a new one. Later, we sit at home and drink vodka and eat *salo* – raw pig fat – and Zhenia's grandmother says cruel things like, "Her sandwiches were disgusting," and "Her cooking was worse than a Moldovan's," and "The cucumbers in her garden were shrivelled."

Half-way through the evening we get a phone call to say that her neighbours have dug up the garden fence and stolen two feet of land.

Zhenia and I drive round to her house to teach the neighbours a lesson.

Grandmother Two dies. I am a rich man. I own a bank and a mansion in Koncha Zaspa. My mother lives in a grand house and has six people working for her. She knows all of them from the village, which makes it extra pleasing to tell them what to do all day. But they need the work. Their sons still live at home and eat soup made from vegetables in the garden.

At the graveyard, the entire village comes to mourn. They are in their best clothes. Many are weeping and they make sure to come personally to me to tell me what a loss she will be to them. They also don't fail to mention how their daughter / granddaughter / niece (always a girl, for some reason) is deadly sick in hospital and will die unless I am so kind as to lend them a thousand hrivnas. My pockets are stuffed with banknotes and I count them out right there and then at the graveside.

Later, we go to the restaurant in the village. I have hired out the whole place so that everyone can share. Tables are laden with salads, meats, fish, caviar, bottles of wine and vodka and cognac. The village feasts and mourns and eats as much as they can. Endless toasts are made to Grandmother Two. My mother has never been happier. She is the queen of the village.

At the end of the night, Zhenia and I drive back to Kyiv. He is in a Bentley; I am in a Maybach.

It is good to be rich.

Francis

Four-thirty a.m.

Nine-thirty at night in London.

Today is the day of Vipassana. The path to enlightenment. The method passed down for twenty-five hundred years from the Buddha, through monks, to me, today.

The clock of Vipassana has struck, we are told. It is time to spread this knowledge throughout the world. It is time to bring it into the light.

Breathe.

Last night, sleepy and stiff from nine hours of meditation, we were taught the method we had come to Thailand to seek. It is so simple, it feels like I could have learned this in the yoga studio in Brixton I went to. Yet there is something very appealing about it.

One day of *anapana*, observing my breath. Two days observing the triangle of my left nostril, my right nostril and the patch of upper lip where the breath falls. And today, I observe my entire body, inch by inch, from the highest point of my scalp, to the extremities of my toes, the length of my back and along my arms to my fingertips. I observe it with a full awareness, as I have observed my nostrils, ready to discover its secrets, the hidden systems that make up my physical self.

Everything is movement, we were told. This is what the Buddha discovered on his journey to enlightenment. He observed his breath and his body with such intensity that he became aware of particles which he called *kalapas*, continually rising and passing away, but rising and passing at such a speed that it made the physical world appear to be solid. He came to understand that, in fact, nothing in the universe was solid. That everything was made up of these quick flashes of rising, disappearing *kalapas* – that everything we think of as solid is in fact in constant movement, in constant transformation.

Everything is changing, we were told. *Anicca, anicca,* rising and passing away.

This is what we observe now, as we focus our minds over the various parts of our bodies. We are experiencing the change. A leg, with shooting pains, cramped and frozen. A scalp, tingling. An arm, gaining moisture. And the pain is gone. Now there is a violent throbbing. On the scalp, itching. On the arms, sweat is running down to the hands.

Everything is changing, we are told. *Anicca, anicca,* rising and passing away.

And we, me, the scientists, discovered this two thousand five hundred years later when we examined atoms. "But it did not bring you happiness," our teacher tells us. "The scientists," (I keep my eyes closed), "did not reach enlightenment, because they looked at the *kalapas* under the microscope. They built giant machines to test their theories. They speculated about the *kalapas*, they wrote about the *kalapas*. But the Buddha, through meditation, experienced the *kalapas*."

And I, changing now, sitting in a meditation hall, observing the top of my head (warm, tingling, crowded with hair, growing sensation), wonder if I, as part of my changing nature, will split into infinite further dualities. Duality of names, nationalities, languages, sexualities, double first in natural sciences, dual states of calm and paranoia, dual states of wanting and not-wanting Jimme in my life, with his frustratingly backward views. Into the future: dual states of self as dedicated meditator and consumer of western extravagance, dual states as man and mind...

...yet it must be more extreme for women, with multiple roles and states. The duality suits men better, this simple structure. Brain or penis. Penis or brain. The path of history can be traced by the decision made within one mind-frame or another...

Alors. I am not observing my body.

I return.

I move downwards.

It will take me all day to reach my toes.

I have nine and a half hours of meditation remaining.

I observe.

The back.

Of my.

Neck.

Itch.

Heat.

I think there is an ant crawling over my shoulder towards it. Observe.

Extreme tickle. I feel its feet moving.

Six feet. Walking over my skin.

I feel each foot.

Do not scratch.

Observe.

It is approaching my neck.

It has stopped.

Extreme itching everywhere.

I can do this.

Breathe.

· · ·

Leila Massey, tall and thin, wearing red, high-heeled boots and a red, woollen dress. Ms. Massey, author of *The Aliens are Invading* and *If It was All True*, hired by the Ministry of Defence to teach us how to anticipate threats.

A snapshot of our laboratory before Leila Massey arrived: fifty scientists, thirty-five women and fifteen men; seventeen PhDs between us, thirty Oxbridge degrees, very little make-up, few smiles.

Leila Massey, writer of science fiction, holder of a degree in literature from Aberystwyth University, wearer of tall red boots, applier of violent red lipstick. Hired to help us do our job.

We sat in the lecture hall, looking up at her extraordinary height. I wondered if she had a special chair and table to write on. I thought, six-foot-three. In comparison, I am five-foot-nine, an average height for a Frenchman, a touch short for an Englishman. Jimme was a stretch taller at five-foot-eleven. Hilary was petite at five-foot-four.

"Good morning, ladies and gentlemen," Leila Massey started. "The key to a great science fiction tale is to make it credible to the reader."

There were many in our department who had been annoyed at having to take the course when we should be in the lab. We had projects to complete to tight deadlines, and this was getting in the way of our real work. There were frowns.

"If we break down science fiction into hard and soft categories, we can see the utopian/dystopian group, which is for the main part political writing; we can see the space operas and grand alien battles group, which is really action/adventure writing. But the most interesting to me, and what we will discuss, is the hard science group. The books that take a current scientific theory or discovery, and build worlds and scenarios around it."

She peered over our faces. "I understand this is what you

already do using extrapolatory methods," she continued. "But I am going to help you go a step further in protecting this country..." she waved her arms around, "and this planet, by plunging into deeper what-ifs, and how we might anticipate them."

Most of us were looking quite interested by now. Some people had even put down their phones. She passed out a reading list as she talked. I glanced at the first two books on it. *The War of the Worlds* by H. G. Wells. A classic. *The Three-Body Problem* by Liu Cixin. I'd never heard of it.

"If something unexpected, extraordinary and catastrophic happens to this planet, the best team to defend against it will be those who have contemplated multiple wild scenarios and brainstormed how to deal with them. That team will have the most flexible thinking, the craziest defence mechanisms in place and will panic the least. If I do my job well in these two weeks, that team will be you."

All phones were down by now. What she said was true. I, for one, was a little pale. If something wild did happen to the planet, who, right now, was the best prepared to deal with it? The Americans, with their excessive force? The British, with their underwater nuclear weapons that probably didn't work anymore? The French? Just thinking back to our French unit made me feel nauseous. It wasn't ready for anything. We were just predicting repetitions of past attacks. We weren't anticipating anything new. Who was on the front line? Right now, it felt like only Leila Massey.

Breathe.

I had observed: the top of my head, my entire scalp, my temples, forehead, nostrils (I no longer counted my nose as one entity), cheeks, ears, the upper lip directly beneath the nostrils, lips, chin, neck, shoulders, top arms, lower arms, top of hands, fingers, palms, chest, stomach, (avoiding the groin, as instructed), thighs, top legs, lower legs, feet (left foot frozen, numb; right foot sharp, painful tingling), upper back, lower back, buttocks.

Time to start again.

Leila handed out pieces of green paper and made us all write down the top three real threats (based on existing knowledge, weapons and states of mind) that we believed were posed against the planet. Then she handed out pink pieces of paper and asked for the top three threats that the planet could face in a hundred years' time.

She collected all the papers and sent us for coffee.

When we returned, she divided us into groups: Wormholes; extra-terrestrial invasion; secretly developed chemical weapons (humans); total annihilation of humans by extra-terrestrial force using weapons we do not know about, with the aim of taking over the planet; space wars; battles on other planets (Mars, to start); time warp / time machines (altering events, people disappearing); other dimensions becoming apparent, with new risks visible.

For a joke, I had written: "World peace leads to extreme boredom. Homo sapiens die out due to lack of conflict."

"Why do we have to look a hundred years ahead?" asked Emma, an Oxford PhD in Microbiology. "I think this is too far. The changes that have taken place over the last hundred years couldn't have been anticipated in the 1900s. It's more useful to look ten to fifty years ahead."

Leila cleared her throat and stepped to the microphone. "The exercise," she said, "is about flexible thinking. You scientists are used to very focused examination of situations and elements. You look into the microscope and you record what you see and you build scenarios based on this. My job is to stretch your thinking wider."

Three weeks later, and all I could see around me was risk.

A month later, and they sent me to Thailand on indefinite leave.

Perhaps some minds are more stretchable than others.

DAY SIX

Laeticia

YESTERDAY WAS a fever of fury and tormented thoughts. After each meditation I splashed cold water over my face and body, but the rage swelled up, over and over, my head saturated with scenarios of revenge and violence.

In the talk at the end of the day, our teachers explained, as if they had seen inside my tortured brain, that our subconscious is filled with sleeping volcanos, which are the memories and hurts of the past, and these volcanos can erupt at any moment and overpower our minds with visions and emotions.

The job of Vipassana is to dissolve these volcanos. Each time these feelings rise to the surface – the fury, the grief, the remorse – we observe the sensations they create on our bodies. Heat, tingling, compression, itching, shaking, burning. We observe, without reaction, and the emotions, the memories, are weakened. We repeat this over and over and the volcanos of hidden pain grow smaller, their power reduced, their fire cooled in the calm of our silent observation.

I was certain that the teachers were speaking directly to me. And yet, what they were describing is a universal affliction. Each meditator in that room was being flooded with eruptions of memory. Each citizen of the earth carries these volcanos in their subconscious. I felt a marvellous gratitude that the teachers were speaking straight to my heart, and also that I was sharing this exquisitely painful process with so many others; in fact, with all of mankind. Eventually, we were told, the sleeping volcanos will have no power at all.

No power at all. Control over my reactions. This is what Anabel wanted for me. This is what I want for myself. I will claim all of myself back. I will recover. I will live a full and empowered life.

Anabel, I will do this for you. I will do this for me.

The sleeping volcanoes will shoot up their memories, and I will observe and not react.

I observe my breath. I observe my body. I observe the sensations on my skin.

I observe the burning when the rape flashes into my mind, the burning and throbbing in my head, goosebumps rising over the skin of my arms, a contraction of my stomach and vaginal passage, a pressure against my eyes.

Again.

The images flash before me, the sensations lift, they burn, they throb, they scream.

I observe. I do not react.

What happened to me was not personal. It was an expression of a society still controlled by men. I was simply a percentage. I was proof of the hypothesis. It was not special. It was deeply unremarkable.

Rage rising.

I observe.

Could the Buddha have achieved such peace if he was a woman?

What if he was raped?

He was a privileged, rich aristocrat with everything in the world. Surely, it's easy to give up riches if you have already tasted everything? You can always say: *Oops, it was a mistake! Just sowing my wild oats with some crazy ideas!* and go back to your rich family.

What if you are a woman who has never had your own power, or opportunity to grow, whose body has been controlled and abused by different oppressors? How can you find peace then?

Is this whole Buddhist peace thing a privileged male excuse to get some time out?

Come on Laeticia. Try.

Let me have a wisp of peace today.

I care.

I care for the human souls in this world.

I care for myself.

I care for my daughter.

I care for Anabel.

I care for the future of the women in this world.

I will re-build my life on terms of happiness and serenity.

I will not carry darkness and hatred and bitterness inside me.

I will expunge the sleeping volcanoes.

I will not let men define me.

I will be whole.

A wisp.

Breathe.

"Promise me you'll say yes."

Anabel was on the phone. It was her fast, clipped New York speech, half-shouted, that reminded me how busy everyone was back in Manhattan, and how loud it always was with the traffic and everyone else shouting.

"I'm not promising that," I replied. I'd stepped outside the café onto the cobbled Paris street.

"I'm insisting, Laeticia," she said. "You know I flew all the way to Paris to help you have that baby. You owe me."

"Tell me what it is."

"I booked you on a course. It's in Thailand. It's meditating. I think it'll help you get over... the thing."

"You know I don't meditate," I countered.

"Laeticia." Her voice was insistent. Her power stare was coming at me though the phone. "We said we were gonna try everything until you were better. Have you done self-defence?"

"No."

"Therapy?"

"No."

"A retreat?"

"I've got a baby and a business to run, Anabel. I've got rent to pay and events to host. You know I don't have time."

"Well, you're making time for this."

Anabel, on the other hand, did meditate.

I found this out one evening, walking back to our halls together from the Columbia University library, where we'd been studying for the next assessment.

I decided to share my mountain theory with her and she got it immediately.

"I feel exactly the same!" she exclaimed. "Like I'm climbing this impossible mountain with everything against me – the weather, the other climbers, the steepness of it, falling rocks, nowhere to rest – the whole thing." She paused. "But weirdly, that only makes me more determined to get to the top and stay there."

"And send down ropes to help other women up," I added.

"I'll help *you* up," she laughed. "But thanks to my mom, I've also got the entire weight of African-American history to carry up that damn mountain. Can you imagine? On top of everything else? If I glance down to see how far I've come, and then feel *that* heaviness on my back? It's too much, Laeticia.

"Don't tell anyone," she said suddenly, squeezing my hand, "but I meditate. For an hour every morning. It's the only time when I can take off that rucksack and get down from the mountain. It frees me. It gives me a brain-rest from the hundred-tonne weight of history I carry round. And from my mom telling me to work harder."

"I've tried it once or twice," I said hesitantly.

"I couldn't get by without it," Anabel continued. We'd reached the building where our rooms were located and stopped at the entrance, a sudden warmth between us.

"It helps me with the power stare as well." She fixed her piercing eyes on me and, as usual, I felt the strength drain out of my body and a helpless desire to do anything she might tell me to.

"If you start meditating, I'll teach you the stare." She softened her eyes and the smile returned. "Now, time to study."

Her power stare also served her in the classroom. Most of the international relations students were white, so Anabel and I stood out immediately. I was six-feet of Brazilian gold, and she was five-feet-ten of African-American curves, brains and searing eyes, with a different hairstyle each week. Sometimes it was bright red curls, sometimes straight and sleek navy blue, sometimes cornrows and thin plaits. Whatever the style was, she would draw everyone's eye with her height and that stare.

We found the other students prudish and earnest – thinking deeply, but not wide enough. They tried, but you could see the mental prisons they were entrenched in. Everything they had been taught had been white, and while they could go a few paces beyond that space, they were constantly drawn back to the default *rightness* of it.

Whiteness had never been my reality, growing up in Rio, and from Anabel's perspective it was just wrong, so we were far more able to understand the aversion of the non-western world to following the rules of the hegemonic US world order or why the Chinese populace would accept authoritarianism in the name of stability after decades of revolution and famine. This understanding pushed our grades that bit higher.

"I'm serious," she said again, before we pushed the door open to go back to our rooms. "Don't tell anyone about the meditating. It's my superpower."

"No way," I said. "Now I know we're both up on this mountain, we've got to look out for each other even more."

She waved the textbook at me. "Now go study," she said. "I'll see you tomorrow."

Ivan

I am back.

I came to breakfast this morning and when I had finished eating, an administrator pointed to the line of meditators walking towards the hall and nodded.

At least they practice their forgiveness principle. What's the use in a programme like this if you start off perfect, right?

So, here I am. They sat me on the edge though, at the back. I guess the administration is on high alert in case they need to hustle me out of here – in case I start pushing and punching the meditators. Well, let them worry.

From here I can see the entire hall. I can see most of the women across the thick white line. I can see the monks on the far left but I don't see my monk. Is he there? Has he gone? Was he a figment of my imagination? I see the teachers at the front on the raised platform. That's where they explain our meditation goals for the day and where they play the S. N. Goenka video. I like this Goenka and his soft voice. I think he made some good choices. He had a lifetime of luxury and business and married life and children, and then wanted to try something new, so he re-invented himself as a guru. I can respect that. He's been successful too. And he's got a useful product. I feel I could sit down with Mr. S. N. Goenka and share a few glasses of vodka. I'd give him my feedback. "If you start off with one monk," I'd tell him, "you need to stick with the same monk. Don't go switching the monks on the meditators. They'll feel confused and betrayed."

Mr. S. N. Goenka raises his glass to me. "The only betrayal you feel is inside yourself," he says in a wise voice. "You are projecting your own feelings onto the monk. The monk is a mirror for your emotions."

Something dark and painful rises in me when Mr. S. N. Goenka says this. The vodka suddenly looks unappetising.

"Tell me how the monk made you feel," says Mr. S. N. Goenka.

I've never been in a therapy session. And I don't plan to start now. But I'll try. I'll give him a chance. I've come all the way to Thailand, after all.

"I felt betrayed," I say. "I felt hurt. Hurt badly. Like I had given my heart to the monk and he had torn it apart. He threw it away like an ugly first wife. I felt as if I had loved him truly and believed that he loved me too – a brotherly love, you understand? – and then it turns out that the brotherly love was unreciprocated. He didn't care about me. He just let me love him, like a fool. Then I was left stranded with my heart open and he trod on it by sending another monk to me. As if there was no difference."

Mr. S. N. Goenka takes a deep breath. I take a deep breath also. I wonder if I am crying again. I wonder if they'll come and throw me out of the meditation hall.

"My question to you," he says, "is are you ready to heal this situation?" He opens his palms to me and we sit, facing each other cross-legged, with his words between us.

I look at the glass of vodka. I don't want to drink it anymore.

"I think that's why I'm here," I say.

. . .

They are telling us that we are over halfway. I wonder what I missed yesterday. I'm enjoying the teaching, strangely. It's straightforward. *Observe the sensations on the surface of your body,* they say. *Whatever comes into your mind has a reaction on your skin.*

So, I start at the top of my head and it is aching, as usual, a dull ache right through my skull, pulling my face and brain downwards. Hangover accumulation, as I think of it. Then the neck: throbbing and sweating. Then the shoulders: itching. Then the arms: throbbing, itching, tickling, sweating.

The sensations are not pleasant, but I know that what's in my mind is not pleasant. It reminds me of why I came here. Somehow, I am enjoying the silence and sitting in a quiet room. My life has been so loud!

Of course, it would help if I could stop spontaneously crying. Let's carry on.

Trunk: hot and sweating. Lower back: a strong, dull ache. Legs: itching and sweating. Knees: shards of white pain stabbing into them at two- or three-second intervals. Calves: low-level aching. Right foot: stabbing pain; left foot: that numb feeling that is more like your foot's been left in an ice-box than you actually can't feel anything.

In short: pain.

There. That's the whole body. I'm a long way from physical bliss. I wonder how many of the people in this hall have discomfort all through their body. Maybe everyone here is dealing with mental torment? Everyone has their own journey. Maybe all the women have been beaten up, or all the men have been cheated on. Maybe they've lost their money gambling and have to start from the beginning. That would make it a hall of losers. It doesn't feel like it, though. The people feel calm. Strong. I'm not seeing broken faces. Except for me. I'm obviously broken. Six-foot-four and sobbing every time I'm in public. There had better not be any other Ukrainians here. If word got back to Kyiv, I'd be a laughing stock.

. . .

"Okay, Mr. S. N. Goenka," I say. "What's the answer? I'm hurt and betrayed. My heart's bleeding and I'm blaming it on your monks. How do I fix this so I can go back to my happy, old life of earning vast amounts of money and having sex with many beautiful women?"

Mr. S. N. Goenka has a twinkle in his eye. "Yes," he replies. "It feels good when the world's your oyster."

I raise the glass of vodka. "To the old," I say. We knock it back.

Mr. S. N. Goenka puts his head on one side. "You won't tell the monks I drank that, will you?" he asks. "They would be shocked."

The mood in the meditation hall has changed. It's calmer. Deeper. The breathing is longer. I can see some faces and they're far away. There is less fidgeting and rustling, scratching and sniffing. The sound of breathing is getting louder. We can hear the jungle better as well. The squawking, the humming, some kind of beating. Or is that in my head? Is it my heart?

"The answer is very simple," Mr. S. N. Goenka says. "So please do not get angry with me when I tell you a simple thing."

He's right – I had tensed myself for his answer. I was already angry. Okay. I breathe. I'm listening.

"You need to forgive yourself," he says. "And you need to forgive him."

Mr. S. N. Goenka pours two more shot glasses of vodka.

We let the words sit.

"Forgive myself?" I say at last.

Now he gives me a stern look. "Just because I have not heard your story," he says. "Does not mean that I cannot see what you have done."

Very well. I was just testing.

"Okay," I say. "But which first? Me or him?"

"You first," he says. "Always you first. Always start with yourself. And finish with yourself. That is your main work – yourself. It is a golden rule," he adds, "if you will forgive the cliché."

I can let a cliché go. "The golden rule," I repeat. "Me, me, me, me, me."

"If you would like to put it in egotistical terms, then yes. It is a good way to remember it." He chuckles. "It is a good joke. I like it. I will share it with my pupils."

I picture him surrounded by his orange-sheeted monks, all chuckling.

"You won't tell them about me?" I growl. "Don't use me as a case study! This is confidential!"

He is about to say something, but then he holds up a finger.

"Brother Ivan," he says. "I would say no, but right now you are not able to trust anyone or anything, due to your excruciating inner pain, which is causing you to weep in public places. If I said those words, then it would spark in your heart memories of believing and then being betrayed, which would lead to anger and then you would possibly hit me with the bottle of vodka."

He is right! I was ready.

He smiles and nods.

"This is the difference between the master and the student," he says. "I am referring, of course, to my pupil-monk who did not carefully think about whether he should approach you in the dining area. He ended up on his rear end on the floor. I would prefer to remain two steps ahead and protect my rear end."

"I think I like you, Mr. S. N. Goenka," I say. "Perhaps you'd be interested in coming back to Ukraine to work for me, after this course is over?"

"Oh, Brother Ivan," he says. "I have taken the vow of sīla. Now, as you know from my nightly lectures, this includes right livelihood. And I suspect that if I came to work for you, I would risk breaking this most sacred vow."

He pauses.

"And also," he continues, "I'd have all your employees meditating and then they'd realise they have full control over their lives and leave to work for a better employer."

"It's a good point," I say. "On second thought, it's better if you stay in Thailand."

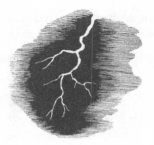

Francis

Four-thirty a.m.

Nine-thirty at night in London.

Cross-legged. Silent. I begin with the top of my head. Tingling. Itching. It's a long way to my toes.

For the last hour I have been catching silent spiders with Tor. He shook my arm in the night, waving his torch in my eyes.

"Hsssss," he said. "Sssssssssss."

"Gnnnnnnnnn," I said. His face was moon-coloured in the torch light. I sat up. He pointed the beam at the ceiling where three spiders were poised. I looked at my watch. Three a.m.

"Gnnnnnnn," I said.

Spiders. The perfect conduit for carrying disease. Large enough for their bodies to bear a significant amount of poison, bacteria or infection. Common enough for nobody in the world to suspect an attack. Easily bred in simple facilities. Two or three could wipe out a room of politicians in minutes. Undetectable if someone was carrying them in a sealed container on their body. A hundred could take down a conference hall.

And if the disease was one introduced by extra-terrestrials, which humans had no immunity to? Surely spiders would be the easiest way to clear the planet for a new habitation?

. . .

"Team E! Extra-terrestrials launching an attack using an instantly fatal disease to which humans have no immunity! Attack is planet-wide! Go!"

Emma (PhD in Microbiology, Oxford University), Shana (Natural Sciences at Cambridge, Queens' College) and me: Team E. Thirty minutes to save the world from alien spiders.

Emma: "Assume the spiders will infect everything not specifically protected."

Me: "What's our goal?"

Shana: "To preserve enough of human life to be able to survive the attack. And to fight back against the infection. And to resist the invaders."

Me: "But even if we could save a few thousand people, if the extra-terrestrials had the planning and skill and technology to launch that attack, then they could easily take out the remaining humans. It won't be like a film where we hunker down and defeat them. They'll just come for us. In the best-case scenario they'll use us as slaves."

Emma: "So, in this case, we think that there is a zero chance of retaining human hegemony of the planet."

Shana and me: "Yes."

Emma: "Then let's think laterally. What are some other options?"

Shana: "Negotiate. Make sure there are provisions for a few thousand people to remain sealed away and safe from attack. Then open discussions. At the very least they will be highly intelligent. We have no idea how willing they will be to talk to us or keep any of us alive. If they are ready to wipe out the entire planet population then the odds are low."

Me: "It seems that the only chance the human race would have of survival in this scenario is to already have colonies on other planets and to be working towards further colonies. While we are all on one planet, the risk is focused in one place, which is easily destroyed by a species with more advanced technology."

Emma: "Then the only possible survival scenario is for the earth scientists to have already developed the technologies to set up colonies, the cost-effective means to travel to them and _"

Shana: "I think we're being too defeatist. We're saying if extra-terrestrials who want to take over Earth and who have advanced technologies launch an attack, then there is nothing we can do?"

Emma: "Yes. That is my conclusion. Anything we can think of doing, they will already have anticipated. If they are truly advanced then they will have already done extensive research on what defences we have. They will be prepared."

Me: "I think we're only exploring the scenario in which they are highly intelligent and have already covered all bases. This is the worst-case scenario. What if they are merely aggressive and release these disease-spiders on all planets they want to take over? What if we have a chance of fighting back?"

Shana: "Then we need massive sterile facilities that are accessible in minutes, and we need a good proportion of the population carrying biohazard suits."

Me: "Or we need to ensure that a certain number of critical individuals – I mean, a sample of highly intelligent men, women and children, who could carry on the human race and fight a war – are in these safe facilities at any given time and would survive unless the extra-terrestrials knew the locations."

Emma: "I'm still not convinced. Even if we did this, we're taking extreme measures to guard against one possible, quite unlikely threat. The actual attack could come in an entirely different form."

Me: "So we're nowhere."

Shana: "We're not nowhere. We're just going extinct."

Breathe.

. . .

By three-thirty a.m. all the spiders are gone. I go to have a shower.

The moon is huge and the jungle loud, hissing and murmuring in the hot, wet air. I try to estimate how many spiders there are in the jungle. A hundred thousand, I decide. The number should stay fairly steady, with the constant flow of egg-laying and death-by-predator. I observe the water falling on my skin. It makes a hot, pleasant drumming. I focus on it, as I have been focusing on my body in the meditations.

Observe: relief, a temporary sense of calm and the possibility of goodness in the world.

No, that's not a physical sensation.

Try again. Droplets of water striking my body, my skin softening and easing. No. The physical description doesn't capture the gift of modern living. I return to my initial analysis: a temporary belief in the possibility of good things lying ahead for this day. This is the secret of a hot shower.

Breathe.

Jimme is gone. I am sure of it. I will come back and he will have moved out. He will have disappeared from my life with grace and ease. There will be no hurt or remonstrance from him; no regret or pain. Wherever he is, there will be sweet laughter and a joy glowing in his eyes. Long, elegant fingers wanting to teach maths in school. A body so graceful and natural it barely belongs in this modern world of constructs and images.

I could not bear his dishonesty. Or his loyalty. In the end, I couldn't decide which it was: being dishonest to his nature – to the truth of his beautiful self – or being nobly loyal to his family, the ones he loved and was responsible for.

Either way, it was his choice, and it was not a choice I could live with.

"Marry me," I asked him again. "You'll live in England legally and we'll be together. You can bring your family over. You can re-train as a teacher. You'll be respected and won't have to hide anything."

He was looking at me with the happy, veiled eyes. The *yes, Francis, you are a good person with your European values,* eyes.

"We could have children," I carried on desperately. "If you want children, we can find a surrogate. She can have your child. We can bring him up."

His eyes changed then. He began to speak and stopped. He checked himself. But I had seen the flash of emotion in his face. The disgust.

"It is not the way we do this in Uganda," he told me at last. Repeating the old mantra.

I understood. Beneath the easiness and grace, the *joie de vivre* and openness, there was hatred. He hated me. He thought I was disgusting. He hated his own nature.

"Okay, Jimme. I'm going out. I'll see you later."

How can the world possibly protect itself from terrestrial or extra-terrestrial threats when it can't even protect itself from its own patterns of self-hatred?

I walked through the streets of Brixton. It started to rain. The stupidity of the human race made me want to pull lampposts from the pavement and hurl them through windows. Hating ourselves. Hating each other. Destroying ourselves and each other. What was the point of any of it? What a stupid job I had, protecting the human race from itself.

And yet, this was the plot of the second book on our reading list. Humans who had contacted extra-terrestrial civilisations to request they take over Earth. People who were so disillusioned with the human race they asked another species to come and rule it. I could understand this point of view. Except for the fact that the new civilisation would most likely be worse, or would have such a low opinion of humans that we would be enslaved or destroyed.

Is this what we in fact deserve? I simply find it impossible to understand how we can have PhDs and philosophical systems and an understanding of so much of science and can still exist in hatred and fear, not providing basic standards of living for so much of our species. Or am I speaking as a one percent exception of intelligence, and it is the ninety-nine percent of people on Earth creating havoc and misery and enabling this tragic situation where the best use of my double first brain is to protect humanity against itself?

Breathe.

DAY SEVEN

Laeticia

NEAT ROWS.
  Blue cushions.
  White line.
  Breathe.

I see the two men at the far end of the room. I hope they are finding what they came for. I send them a blessing. I send a blessing to every soul in the room, women and men. I send a blessing to the teacher, who is seated on the platform at the front of the room, and the three monks wrapped in orange *kāṣāya* to the far left of the room.

I'm feeling it rise in me, suddenly, unexpectedly – a soapy

gratitude washing other thoughts away. Gratitude for us, here; for me, here; for Anabel never giving up on me; for having Beatriz in my life; for being able to leave her in my mother's safe hands; gratitude that my body was healthy and strong to carry a girl.

And the people in the kitchens doing *seva*, their spiritual service. A blessing on them. Former students who volunteer for days or weeks or months to prepare food and sweep and wash the floor in this room so we might discover the transforming wonder of Vipassana and silence. The jungle just beyond us, magnificent, secret, an impossible construction of multitudinous ecosystems: cycle within cycle of insects, reptiles, mammals, creepers, catchers; primeval fronds and twisting, watching ropes of green living cells. Blessings on you for being inexorably perfect! For not screwing up your environment the way humans do at every opportunity! Wonderful, miraculous jungle. A thousand blessings on you. Not that you need them. You are your own wondrous blessing. Your very existence is a blessing on the planet. You are beneficial in every way. Thank you. Thank you. Thank you.

It's spilling out now. I can't stop it. I'm trying to observe the sensations but I'm filling with excitement and love and my heart is pushing outwards with wonder and gratitude. Is this what happens when you don't speak for six days? Is everyone else feeling it? What about my rage? Where has that gone? I was raped! What about that? Juan! Deceit, betrayal, the rottenness of humankind, the inequality on the streets of Brazil. No. Nothing is helping. The joy is rising steadily in me and it is more powerful than the dark volcanoes that were erupting earlier.

With my eyes closed, I look down on the hall where we're sitting. Neat rows of souls on blue cushions. Orange-clad monks to the side. I see the roof of the meditation hall and the sleeping quarters, the dining room, the entire complex, hidden by secret roads in this jungle clearing. And higher up I see the wide swathe of Thai countryside, hills of jungle and villages and scribbled pathways, then higher and I see the sweep of ocean into semi-circles of land, the white, the green of water, then the silver of cities. And higher, the blur, now, of green and silver and blue as the jungle and ocean and cities disappear into a tiny point. And now I have lost the country, for the globe is turning. What can I make out? Water, water, silver mountains, oh, but if I turn the other way there is... such light...

Breathe.

"Here, just give it a try."

I was in Anabel's room and we were studying for a test later that morning. She hadn't meditated yet and wanted to teach me.

"Tuck your feet into the crooks of your knees, look how I'm doing it. Then sit straight, tighten your abs so your body is tall and proud. Let your hands rest on your thighs. That's it."

We sat facing each other at each end of her bed. The floor of the room was covered with neat piles of books and papers. The desk had pens in rows. The dresser had a line of brushes and curlers.

"Now what?" I asked.

"Close your eyes, breathe, and feel the space up there, above all the day-to-day stuff. Picture all the rushing around we do, then let that go, and take your consciousness higher. You want to be sitting in a place far above that, the place where there's just emptiness. The place where the ideas dance. The place where the genius is glowing. Just go to that place and be there. Exist there. Do nothing. There's nothing to do. Everything you need will come to you there."

Breathe.

. . .

I am in the place where the ideas dance.

I am whole. I am fully awake.

This is my natural state. This is the state I will bring Beatriz up to exist in.

I promise myself, right now, right here, that I will remain in this state. That my life will be spent in this place of female power.

And I promise that I will give myself the tools to stay aware and tingling in this state.

To remain in this place of power I need to be laughing and receptive and green-skirted and flat-shoed.

I need to be filled with poetry and philosophy and paintings.

I need to eat breakfast while dancing, and flirt with strangers.

I need to make love after coffee and sleep naked in her arms.

I need to pay a dozen compliments a day: What hair! What a necklace! How slender! What style! What a photograph! What delicious eggs! What coffee!

I need to thank the goddess every day that I have a daughter.

I need to dance with Beatriz to music and hear her laugh, and laugh with her.

I need to tell Beatriz a story each day that has a brave, successful woman in it.

I need to paint a picture with Beatriz every week and throw the paint against the walls and roll around on the floor with paint in our hair and on our cheeks.

I need to sit with Beatriz and design clothes that I will make her: small cup-cake hats; wide blue trousers; T-shirts with mushrooms and ships on them.

I need to hire a man to do the dusting and mopping.

I need to make love with someone surprising and beautiful each month.

I need to light a candle and sit and watch the flame, and marvel.

I need to buy armfuls of flowers and fill the apartment with colours; and teach Beatriz the smells and the names.

I need to eat oysters every week.

I need to wear red lipstick once a month.

I need to have a glass of wine in a bar on my own and savour it as if it is the one Anaïs Nin has just bought me.

I need to re-read the books of Anaïs Nin.

I need to hear about the life of my mother, and I don't mean the part where she married my father, I mean the life! The dreams and the secret parts in between, what she whispered to her sister and her girlfriends and into the pillow.

I need to explain to my mother my vision for Beatriz, this child of light.

I need to explain to my mother why Beatriz cannot wear pink, unless it is mixed with green and stars and matched with a mushroom beret.

I need to stroke myself to delirious pleasure and savour every moment of it. Perfume myself, brush my hair, shave my legs, fix on some jewellery and a brassiere with lace. Moan as loudly as I can and make sure the neighbours know that I am alone.

I need to climb a tree and sit among the leaves, breathing, green, alive.

Ivan

Zhenia and I.

We are in a hotel room.

We have forced someone to sign over a business to us and now they are here, in the hotel, with a gun. One of our bodyguards is dead and we don't know where the other is. It's just me and Zhenia in the room.

Zhenia is always one step ahead. It's his speciality. It's how we have stayed alive so far. But he didn't see this coming. He's sitting on the end of the bed and he has his innocent face on. He's scared. It's not a good sign. He's not thinking anymore.

"It's my fault, Vanya," he says, "I set it up so he would think Boris had done it. I thought it would work. But Boris was killed yesterday so now it's impossible for Boris to have done it. It made it clear as the day that we did it. I've messed up."

"Zhenichka," I say. I'm sitting in the armchair, straight-backed. I'm ready for gunfire to come through the door. "Zhenichka, we're not dead yet, just like Ukraine." I quote the Ukrainian national anthem – it's a poem by Taras Shevchenko, and an old joke of ours. *Ukraine is not yet dead* is the first line. It's how we start anything dangerous. *"Shshe ne vmerla,"* I repeat. We're not dead yet.

Zhenia nods. His face is white. You wouldn't even believe he could do the sneaky face if you saw him like that. "I'm sorry, Vanya," he says. "If we die, I'm sorry. It was my mistake."

"We're not going to die," I say forcefully.

"Katya will be alright," he says. "I've set her up. She's got bank accounts and assets. She'll be fine. She can hide for a while."

There is the sound of shooting somewhere in the hotel. It's on a different floor. The drum of boots running. These may be our last minutes. There's something I need to know.

"Zhenia. How did you persuade Katya to marry you?"

He understands why I'm asking this question. He understands I could only ask it with bullets flying around us.

He answers me, with his white, innocent, scared, small-boy face. "I told her I'd give her freedom," he says. "I told her I would get her to America, where she would be free. And rich." Now he is speaking the words into the space above my shoulder. "I told her you could give her your love, but you couldn't give her that."

He says the words, and I know there are no other earthly circumstances where he would have spoken them and they would have been true.

I find it hard to breathe. I could have had her. She could have been my wife. I hear boots running. Should I let them shoot me dead? Should I let them shoot Zhenia dead? I look at his face. It is white-green. It has stretched. It is wider. It is a giant cheese. It is a sweating moon. It is a ball of fear.

I want to grab his little neck and rip that face off his disgusting little head. I want to punch my fist into it until all the insides spill out over his shoulders. Then I'll return him to Katya.

"He was mistaken," I'll inform her. "He told you I could not give you everything you desired. But I am here to correct the mistake."

I throw his body out onto the street and Katya and I never

speak of it again. We are married and have four children. They are tall and beautiful. Some have green eyes, some have blue. Our youngest girl has one of each colour.

"Vanya." Zhenia chokes the word out. "*Proshai.*"

One word: forgive. Small, simple word. *Proshai.*

Never, I say to myself.

There is a hard knocking on the door.

"Ivan Ivanovich, it's clear." The voice of my bodyguard. "He's dead. You can come out. We should get away from the hotel. The car is waiting."

Now is the time for a decision. The room is filled with this one word. It's throbbing, it's expanding: *proshai.*

Never, I say to myself again. I swallow it down. Never.

I turn to Zhenia. His face is yellow now. My face is stone. "*Po-shli*," I say. "Let's go. We're alive."

"So, Mr. S. N. Goenka, you would have me forgive myself first? Well, let's look at original sins, shall we? Let's trace the line of betrayal back to the first act."

Mr. S. N. Goenka smiles at me and nods.

"Do you remember stealing his sandwiches at kindergarten?" he asks.

"What?"

"Come, don't play stupid. He had two caviar sandwiches for lunch. His grandmother had wrapped them up for him. Thick butter and red caviar. You stole them."

I can't deny it. I see myself unwrapping them and eating them as fast as possible. His grandmother made good sandwiches. My grandmother always put tongue on mine. Tongue or liver. And never enough butter.

"He didn't mind," I say. "He didn't even like caviar that much. His grandmother made him a good breakfast."

"He was hungry," says Mr. S. N. Goenka. "Because of you, he was hungry at school."

"Fine," I say. "Is that why he stole Katya?"

"Is Katya something that can be stolen?" he asks.

I had not thought he was an idiot before. Maybe I'm wasting my time on a simpleton.

"Yes," I reply. "Of course."

Forgiveness.

What does it mean when there's so much to forgive? The pile is so high it's difficult to see through it.

This is what I forgive myself for:

Lying to my mother; lying to my grandmother; stealing from the house; stealing from the school; stealing Zhenia's caviar sandwiches; stealing businesses from people who had stolen them from someone else; cheating on Eva; sleeping with Katya; siphoning money from all of Zhenia's businesses.

But if I hadn't done all those things, I wouldn't be the man I am today. I'd be a failure. I'd be working in one of the factories. I'd be dead. I'd be married to someone who looked like my grandmother.

Okay. That didn't work.

Let's try the other way round.

This is what I forgive Zhenia for:

Stealing Katya. Never. Arranging to have me voted out of my business so I lose all control. Maybe. Stealing Katya. Never.

Mr. S. N. Goenka: "It seems we have come to the root of the problem."

Me: "It seems so."

Mr. S. N. Goenka: "If you can forgive him for taking Katya by stealthy means, then we can move on and forgive all the other areas."

Me: "That will never happen. But yes, your logic is not incorrect."

Mr. S. N. Goenka: "Tell me what Katya means to you."

Me: "Katya is all that is true and beautiful in life. She is the best and the most pure. She is the ultimate prize. Every student in school wanted her. Every teacher in school. Every man that has ever seen her has wanted her."

Mr. S. N. Goenka: "So she is an object to attain?"

Me: "Yes."

Mr. S. N. Goenka: "Tell me about what she is like. Her personality."

Me: "She is hard and smart and ruthless. She is a survivor. She is a woman of the times. She does not make mistakes – apart from marrying Zhenia and believing his lies. She knows the importance of money. She knows the importance of loyalty and being able to prove who has fathered your children. She understands men such as me and Zhenia. She comes from the same place. Her father was a miner. Her mother was an accountant. She is part of us. She knows us. She understands why we need her. She understands why no other woman will truly satisfy us."

Mr. S. N. Goenka: "Explain that to me."

Me: "Eva, for example. She is beautiful, smart, funny. Graduated from university with a degree in biology. She plans to open a business. Her family is good. She grew up in Kyiv in a nice flat. She likes money and being rich. She's young and sees hope for our country."

Mr. S. N. Goenka: "And Katya?"

Me: "Katya knows the dark, dreadful depths that Zhenia and I went to, to get where we are today. She knows Zhenia and I nearly died many times stealing businesses. She knows what we started from. She knows I stole Zhenia's caviar sandwiches. She knows how dry the tongue on my own sandwiches was. She knows how we never looked at another girl in all our years at school. She knows why we didn't go to university. She knows why we'll never trust anyone but each other. She's a part of us."

Mr. S. N. Goenka: "It seems we have a stalemate."

Me: "If you hadn't switched the monks, we wouldn't even be having this conversation."

Mr. S. N. Goenka: "Let's not play the blame game, now. We're here to find solutions. Let's clear out your mind and that will open space for some new approaches to the situation. How does that sound?"

Me: "It sounds more constructive than stalemate."

Mr. S. N. Goenka: "Now we're talking."

Francis

Four-thirty a.m.

Nine-thirty at night in London.

"Wormhole team," Leila Massey called from the front of the room. "What have you got?"

Mohammad stepped forward. "To summarise our discussions, if a wormhole appears near Earth, we have no control over what comes out of it. It could be a curious space explorer – although even a single space explorer could pose a threat to the safety of the planet if their biosystem is non-compatible with elements of the earth's biosphere. It could also be an entire invading army. It could be a single extra-terrestrial with advanced weaponry. It could be a peace delegation."

"So how do you protect Earth from any one of those?" Leila was in green boots today. She must have been a foot-and-a-half taller than Mohammad.

"The only way to do it is to surround the wormhole with a fleet of our spaceships."

There was a discontented noise from the other three members of his team.

"No, I take that back," he said. "There's no way at all of protecting ourselves from anything that might come out of a wormhole, as their technology would be so far advanced if they had been able to find, stabilise and travel through a folded-up piece of space-time."

"So?" Leila raised her shoulders.

"Our conclusion is: the best thing we can do is get back in the research labs and improve our own technology as fast as possible so we can locate and learn about wormholes ourselves and not be surprised by an invading army walking out of one."

"You guys aren't very hopeful," Leila commented.

"That's because we're scientists, not writers," Mohammad answered curtly. "We can only work with what we actually have."

"But let's go back to that," Leila replied. "If some extra-terrestrials did emerge from a wormhole close to Earth, then you and all the world's top scientists would be huddled in a room figuring out what to do. You'd have to take some action. You wouldn't be saying, *let's go back into our labs for two hundred years and then talk to them*. So – let's give it another shot. You've got two hours to make a recommendation to the government on what action to take. Go!"

Sixty-four men meditating around me, and on the other side of the white line, sixty-four women, all of us looking for peace. My eyes travel to the robed figure, rising tall in the sackcloth hood, but as ever there are no clues; he remains hidden in his cavern of penitence. The fidgeter behind me is scratching today, yesterday he was coughing and sneezing, but I now find it calming. His constant movements help to ground my location in this room of strangers. The man-bun beside me is working hard and I feel intense concentration emanating from his poised form.

Across the white line, my eyes seek out the coiled woman, as I have thought of her, and I observe her posture has changed. I don't sense tension now so much as compressed power; she is taller, straighter, more serene. I skim the other faces and feel the sense of peace from the closed figures; the sound of the turning fan; the sound of breathing.

. . .

After the Leila Massey sessions, our entire department was put on computer modelling of extra-terrestrial threats. Most of my colleagues found it an interesting exercise, genuinely sparked by Leila's passion. I had a problem, though. Every scenario I ran ended in the annihilation or subjugation of the human race.

"Your assumptions are too pessimistic." My supervisor had come to my desk to understand what was happening. She had been reviewing the scenario outcomes and was surprised with the end-of-the-world pattern issuing from my computer.

"I think they're overly positive, to be honest," I told her. "All we've got are nuclear weapons. If they don't work, then it's game over every time."

"Look at the *War of the Worlds* scenario," she replied. "Only humans are entirely suited to life on Earth. The Martians were extinguished by common bacteria."

"I have to disagree," I said. "If they are intelligent enough to have the invading technology, they will have done a full bio-analysis of the planet."

"It's a mistake we ourselves could make on a foreign planet," she argued.

I shrugged. Her position was to assume the extra-terrestrials would be as primitive as us. There was no way I was using that as a central premise.

She was looking at me strangely. I wasn't sure why, and then I caught a reflection of myself in the computer screen. My head was shaking quickly and continuously from side to side and I was blinking fast. I realised that I was incredibly cold.

"Please can I lie down?" I asked her.

Ten minutes later, I was huddled in a corner of the laboratory with a blanket wrapped around me.

"It's alright, Francis," someone was saying. "There's a taxi on the way. Take nice deep breaths now."

. . .

Hilary held me in a hug for a long time.

"It's so good to see you, Frenchie!" she said. "I feel like I never see you since we left Cambridge. It's silly we're in the same city and not meeting up more. We should have a monthly dinner at the very least."

"I'd love that," I said. "I want you to meet Jimme."

We sat in the booth of an old London pub, ancient casks hanging over the bar and decades of initials carved into the wooden panelling. Hilary brought us pints of ale while I watched her two-year-old son, happily distracted with crayons and sheets of paper. He was covering the blank pages with many-coloured spiders.

"He's obsessed with bugs," explained Hilary, returning with the drinks. "And now, tell me everything." She spilled some ale onto the table in front of me. "What's gone wrong? How can I help? Why are you going to Thailand?"

It was one of those impossible questions to answer: *What's gone wrong?* So simple – too simple. My mind automatically started going back – *what had gone wrong?* – before Leila Massey, before Hartbridge; was it Paris? Was it Cambridge? Was it boarding school? Was it my father? Was it me? (Of course it was me!) Was it…?

"I remember when I was about seven," I began, letting the memory form the words. "I read a book that my father had given me, a story where the children were cruel and the grown-ups had lied – some cautionary tale. But the book stayed with me and I couldn't sleep for weeks. I remember my mother sitting by my bed every night calming me down and telling me it was just a story."

I lifted the pint glass from its puddle on the table, but set it down again. I could feel the touch of my mother's hand on my forehead.

"And then I found science," I continued. Hilary's glass was covering her mouth, but her eyes were watching my face closely. "And science was nice, clear facts that were not cruel and didn't betray or lie. Science was the truth behind the world... in contrast to the noise and nonsense of human illusion."

I paused. In our Cambridge days, Hilary would have jumped to argue that point back at me, quoting Greek classics and ancient civilisations. Now, she was silent. She waited. I struggled to continue the thought.

"Science was safe for me," I said at last. "And now, science isn't safe for me. Now humans have ruined science for me. With their cruelty... and their lies... and their selfishness..."

I was crying. I pushed the pint glass forward and back through the puddle. I looked over at Hilary's son. He was staring at me, fascinated. His hand rested on his page of spiders. Perhaps he'd never seen a man cry. I met Hilary's eyes.

"I don't see any hope," I said.

My supervisor put me in the taxi herself. She'd looked up my address.

"Is there someone at home to take care of you?" she asked.

I wasn't quite sure where I was or what was going on by then. I was shaking hard and wearing a blanket and my supervisor was in a mother's role with her arm around me. But suddenly I was desperate to answer her question.

"My husband is waiting for me," I said. "He will take care of me."

As I said it, my head switched from shaking to nodding intently.

My supervisor slammed the taxi door and had a word with the driver. Then she leaned through the passenger window.

"We'll check on you tomorrow, Francis," she said. "We think

you might need a leave of absence. We'll talk soon. Don't come into work tomorrow. You need a break. I'll phone you."

"Francis," Hilary said, "you realise you're having a bona fide existential crisis?" She reached out her hand to me, and was clasping my fingers in the puddle of ale. I pushed aside the glass. She'd never called me Francis before. That meant it was bad. I looked up to her eyes and was startled by the compassion in them.

"You're a lovely person, Francis," she said, squeezing my fingers. "I really value you. The more into real life I go, the more I see selfish, rotten people being shallow and not connecting or listening – and I'm not *just* talking about my husband –" her voice dropped to a whisper momentarily. "You always listened to me. You always respected me. You're a beautiful person Frenchie, and I love you."

I smiled at her. They were sweet words, although they wouldn't help solve my predicament.

"You know what they used to call me in Paris?" I asked. "They called me *the English*." Hilary was drinking from my glass of ale now, so I continued. "They thought I wasn't manly because I wouldn't approach a woman in a forthright way, or pinch anyone's bottom or buy drinks that weren't asked for. I wouldn't sleep with anyone who was married or anyone who was drunk. It just didn't make sense to me. It was all so disrespectful. But the French thought there was something wrong with me, especially the women. In the end, they decided it was my prudish English side. So that was my name – *the English*."

"But they said it in French or English?" Hilary asked. "*L'Anglais* perhaps?"

"No – *the English*. It was more insulting like that, I think."

"I thought you had a tonne of sex in Paris?" Hilary questioned. "You told me you did."

"Once they'd figured me out," I replied. "Then I was somewhat of a curiosity. A prize even. Yes, there was plenty of sex in the end."

"Well, maybe your respect tactic will catch on," Hilary laughed. "Women will find it an aphrodisiac. And men," she added quickly.

"That's a whole different game," I said. "There's more of a natural understanding between men."

"Francis," Hilary said, sounding serious now. "I can see you're not okay. I'm so sorry you're not okay. Do you know you've been blinking really fast all the time we've been in the pub? I can see something needs to change. But I just want to say that you might be the last good person left on this planet, and I'm really happy I know you."

It was classic Hilary. Reassuring and unnerving. Loving, but leaving for somewhere else soon after. Full of kind words, but none that resulted in practical solutions. For her, the riches of ancient civilisations were enough to carry her through. I was happy that the foundation of her happiness was in such abundant supply.

But it was not enough for me.

Breathe.

DAY EIGHT

Laeticia

IMAGE: My mother's face. She is standing over a bowl of steaming washing-up in the kitchen. She is wearing a flowered apron and yellow rubber gloves. She is looking over her shoulder towards me and Papa and laughing. Her dark brown hair is pinned up in the formal manner she wears it, but it has come loose from the steam and hot water.

Image: My first sight of Beatriz, placed in my arms by the nurse at the hospital. Her face is squashed. Her hair is black. Her skin is red-brown. Her eyes are long and closed. Her limbs are folded with fat.

Image: Anaïs Nin is sitting in the corner of my café. She is wearing an open-neck shirt and her hair is smoothed back from her face. She is watching. She is thinking. She takes a cigarette from behind her ear and stands up.

Flash: The parliament of Brazil has passed a law mandating that fifty percent of senior positions in any company are to be held by women.

Flash: Beatriz is stepping out of her black executive car. She is tall in flat heels and carries a briefcase. She is C-suite level in a major energy company. She is paid vast amounts of money and most of her employees are women.

Flash: They have cleaned up the seas and oceans.

Flash: The energy at Beatriz's company is one hundred percent renewable.

Flash: The end of the night at the café. The final song of the Toulouse Gypsy Swing Band. Spilled drinks are on every surface. The staff are on the dance floor, some in aprons, the chef in her tall white hat. My hair is wild and flying. The sleeves of my dress are dark with perspiration. Poetry is everywhere.

Flash: Anaïs Nin takes my wrist and brings it to her mouth. She kisses it tenderly.

Flash: Anaïs Nin collapses onto the pillows of my bed. "Why is it always better with women?" she asks, bursting into giggles.

A drive through Brazil. We start at our house. Trees lining the pavement with dancing shadows. Girls and boys on bicycles. Houses, small but individual. Driving further, we reach narrower streets, cafes on pavements, sound – music, shouting, dogs barking. Then the centre: huge billboards, masses of bodies, reflected metal, flash, flash, flash; out of the centre, the other side of the city, men on the streets, quick, suspicious glances, Mama locks the internal car doors, Papa runs two red lights, small houses merge into blocks of flats, vast living spaces, more dogs barking; he checks the mirror – "Is that a gun?" – and we're turning onto the freeway, driving, driving, huge signs overhead – Brasilia, São Paolo – suddenly we're on the coast road, I see the ocean sweeping towards me, away from me, towards me; driving, closer to it, further from it; driving.

At the crossroads, a man with one leg hops up to the car and knocks on the window. "Don't open it, Maria," says Papa. My mother opens it and gives him some money.

At the gas station, a woman with a baby wrapped to her chest approaches. "Maria," says Papa. My mother gives her some money.

"It could be us," Mama says, and Papa looks angry.

Image: My mother poised above the ironing board. Her face is brown from sixty years of sunshine. Her forehead and eyes are creased with folds of skin. Her visage shines with make-up and sweat from the sun and the heat of the iron. Her hair is dark with gleaming silver threads. Her face is at peace. Her body rocks from side to side as she moves the iron over the cloth.

"I got a scholarship to the university," I say in English.

"*J'ai eu une bourse pour l'université,*" I say in French.

"*O que? O que você está dizendo, querida?*" she answers me in Portuguese.

"I've been accepted at the university," I reply, in Portuguese. "I'm going to study foreign relations and languages."

My mother's smile lifts. She turns the shirt. She spreads out the collar.

"You are so clever," she says. "You are such a hard worker. You will be our president," she says.

She smooths the collar of Papa's shirt and irons the edges, holding it straight with her fingertips.

"There are challenges, as a woman," she says, her face still focused on the fabric. "It will not be equal. It will not be an easy path."

"Yes, Mama," I say.

What does she know? What has she seen? What combination of small failures has brought her calm face to this ironing board? What were *her* dreams?

She sighs and picks up the shirt. She shakes it out and examines it at arm's length. She nods, then reaches for a hanger and slips it over. She hooks it onto the rack of ironed garments and fastens the top button.

"Your father needs some new shirts," she says. "These are getting old."

She gets up in the morning and makes a cup of strong coffee for Papa. She brings it to him in bed at six-thirty and wakes him up. Then she prepares breakfast for him. It is on the table at six-fifty. He finishes his shower and dresses and then eats breakfast. She lays the newspaper next to his plate. She does not bother him with chatter.

Image: Beatriz is standing in a kitchen. The windows are clean and light is pouring in. Her hair is tied back in a ponytail. It is long and soft and shining. In her hand is an iron. She is ironing her husband's shirt.

"Is this okay?" she asks me. She holds it up for me to see. The collar is crisp and flat.

She takes a casserole from the oven. She holds it out to me.

"Taste it!" she says. "I think it's the best one I've made. I added some spices to the recipe."

Image: No one can swim in the oceans now because they are full of plastic and rubbish. Everything is polluted. The planet is dying. The men are making as much money as they can before the whole thing goes bust.

Image: Beatriz falls back onto the bed, her fingers still clasped in those of her lover. She is crying. "Jesus," she says.

"Jesus. I didn't know it could be like that." Her lover rolls over on top of her. Their breasts push together. Her lover moves her hand downwards. "I'm not done yet," she says.

Image: Beatriz stands before a packed lecture hall. Over seventy percent of the hall are women. Her hair is grey and pulled back in an unflattering plait. Wire-rimmed glasses sit on her nose.

"Herstory is a series of choices," she says. "For a long time, the choice was a simple one: accept or not accept. Be inside or be outside. Be safe or be in danger. Now, we have more layered choices, ones with more nuance and more possible outcomes. It is easier to make the choices, but it is harder to predict the results."

A young man in the lecture theatre puts up his hand.

"Yes?" she says.

"Would you say the inverse has happened in the case of men's choices?" he asks. "Have our choices now been boiled down to: with them or against them, in any given situation? Previously, all our choices were made inside the system, but now you have become the system so is it our choices that are on trial?"

"Our," repeats Beatriz from the lectern. "Them. We. Our."

A female student turns round to the speaker. "You're using the language of opposition," she says. "You need to see women as the 'us'. Unless you align yourself with women and we are all in the same situation together, then the situation will not resolve, it will just invert."

"That's what I was trying to say," says the young man.

Image: Beatriz pulls off the yellow washing up gloves and wipes her face. She checks the shirt she has ironed for the next morning. The collar is crisp. She opens the oven and pulls out the casserole. She removes the lid and tastes it. The best yet. She takes a plate from the cupboard and spoons out a serving which she carries to the table. She switches on the radio and starts to eat.

Image: Beatriz is being elected President of Brazil. Her vice president squeezes her eyes to stop the tears. She knows what strength and sacrifice it has taken to achieve this.

Beatriz stands. Her eyes skim over the faces of the women in the chamber, her supporters. An image of her grandmother comes to her. The photograph that her mother kept by her bed. Her grandmother is looking back over her shoulder and laughing. She is wearing yellow washing-up gloves and her face is sheened with sweat.

Beatriz begins the oath.

Ivan

I am an orange-robed monk in a Thai temple. I breathe in peace. I breathe out peace.

I am a spider in the jungle. I am small and strong and deadly. You do not see me. I kill you and then feast on you.

I am born a generation earlier. I work all my life in a factory and a coal mine. When I am sixty, the Soviet Union falls, my pension disappears and I have nothing.

I am born a generation later. My parents have stolen enough money for me to have a good life. I study business at university and emigrate to America. I have two children who learn about the Soviet Union in history class and don't speak Russian. They are embarrassed by their parent's heavy accents and halting English.

I am born when I am born. My parents lose everything when I am twenty. The country is up for sale. There are no jobs. All the factories are closed. All I have is strength and cunning. Strength and cunning are the characteristics needed to succeed. I take businesses and turn them around. I start a bank. I make a vast amount of money. My mother lives in one of my houses and has six people working for her.

. . .

My best friend and I love the same woman. He wins her with the promise of America, but ten years later she is still in Kyiv and she lets me sleep with her for a small fortune. My best friend finds out and arranges for me to lose control of all my business holdings. I love him and trust him and so I sign the papers which seem to confirm I am increasing my stake in one company, when in fact it means that my overall stake is below fifty percent and I lose my voting rights. I am voted out of any control by the other shareholders.

My blood pressure goes through the roof and I nearly have a heart attack. My wife thinks I am going to die and talks me into going to Thailand to sit in silence for ten days without my mobile phone.

Mr. S. N. Goenka: "It's a good summary. Nice and succinct. Without emotion. I think you have made solid progress. You are seeing things clearly."

Me: "The breathing helps with that. And the silence. And not being on my phone."

Mr. S. N. Goenka: "Perhaps you would consider doing this every year. It would be beneficial for you to evaluate where you are in terms of your goals and life path."

Me: "Thank you. I'll consider it."

Mr. S. N. Goenka: "Do you see the solution yet?"

Me: "I see why Zhenia did it. And I see why I did what I did to make him do it. I also see why he did the initial thing that started it all."

Mr. S. N. Goenka: "The initial thing?"

Me: "He won Katya by lying to her."

Mr. S. N. Goenka: "How do you feel about that now?"

Me: "I feel embarrassed. Could she be so easily won by a lie? Why didn't I try it? Is Zhenia really more brave and sneaky than me? He used the tactics that worked so successfully for stealing businesses to win a woman. Now I think of it, he used them before we even started stealing together. It makes me think he is the mastermind behind our entire success. Perhaps everything was down to him. Perhaps I am the one who got lucky by being his friend while his brains made us both rich."

Mr. S. N. Goenka: "Well, what do you think you brought to your partnership?"

Me: "In fact, maybe I deserve nothing. It should all belong to Zhenia. The women, the businesses, the money. If it wasn't for him, I'd be outsmarted and dead. I wouldn't be here."

Mr. S. N. Goenka: "Perhaps you are being too harsh on yourself?"

Me: "I see it all clearly now. It was always his. It was I who got lucky. Zhenia taking away my businesses now is his way of showing me that. He is reminding me that he is always three steps ahead."

Mr. S. N. Goenka: "He wasn't ahead when Katya made her proposition to you."

Me: "I don't even know that. Maybe he wanted to test me. Maybe he wanted to set me up. Maybe he's bored of Katya and told her to earn some extra money for herself."

Mr. S. N. Goenka: "So, what do you bring to the relationship, if Zhenia is so far ahead on all counts?"

Me: "I..."

Mr. S. N. Goenka: "Perhaps he loves you?"

I am a spider in the jungle. I am the size of a human fist. I have black hair on my legs and body. I carry venom that can stop the heart of a bird in ten seconds. I eat flesh.

I sleep in a burrow of leaves and silk at the base of a Banyan tree. I do not bring my food into the nest. I feast and then I return to my lair.

At night, I emerge from my burrow. I sense the world around me through the hairs on my legs. I know the tread of larger animals from across the jungle, reverberating into my body; the drip of condensation from the overhanging leaves telling of the heat; the rush of air ahead speaking of a monkey or flying squirrel soaring from tree to tree. It is the language of life and death. It is the language of feeding and being fed upon. The vibrations on my body tell me what danger approaches and what prey is near.

The sound waves inform me that another of my kind is hunting close to my nest. I feel my venom gland cool behind my eyes, throbbing in anticipation, and a quiver runs from my venom canal to my fangs. I am ready to hunt. I move through the leaves, keeping cover beneath them. I am fast if I spot prey. I am fast if there is threat. A drop of condensation drips onto the ground. I crawl forward and drink. The jungle is awake.

Me: "What?"

Mr. S. N. Goenka: "I said, maybe he loves you."

Me: "What do you mean?"

Mr. S. N. Goenka: "I mean like a brother. Does he have a brother?"

Me: "No. Only child."

Mr. S. N. Goenka: "Then perhaps you are his brother. Do you see him as your brother?"

Me: "Yes. I suppose so. Yes, I do."

Mr. S. N. Goenka: "Then there is your answer. Maybe he is responsible for the strategy that made you both rich. But you have been by his side. You have been his companion. In a friendship like that, love builds steadily."

Me: "Then why did he try to destroy me?"

Mr. S. N. Goenka: "Brothers fight. You took an action. He took an action. It does not negate the love. You have the opportunity now, however, to choose your next action carefully. You are in the space between the action and the reaction. You can evaluate past events, the desires of your heart and the possible effects of your next move."

Me: "What do you think would hurt him the most, Mr. S. N. Goenka?"

Mr. S. N. Goenka: "Ivan. Please focus."

Me: "Yes. I apologise. You just said I could do anything."

I identify my prey ahead of me, half-camouflaged in the curled, sticky leaves of a striped plant. It is a wet frog, shining and green. It would be delicious, full of juice and flesh beneath the tough skin. Its hearing and movement sensors are highly developed but its real power is in its flying leap and lightning-fast tongue. I approach from the side. My eight legs glide over adjoining leaves. It only takes one bite. The frog is waiting and watching. I see it focused on a haze of insects approaching. In a few moments it will prepare to jump, flying out towards them with tongue extended, suctioning a fat mouthful before landing to savour its catch. The hairs on my limbs are erect, my body is poised with anticipation of liquefied green flesh. I am so close. So close. The frog is moving back into the pre-jump. I am near enough. I dart forward. *Snap!* My fangs sink into the frog-flesh and my gland of venom is emptied into its body. The frog jerks forward, beginning its leap, but it knows something has changed. The flash of pain; its limbs are not moving smoothly through the air; its limbs are not moving at all; now it cannot move its limbs. It is falling, falling, its heart is slowing, slowing, it is attempting final lashes of head and tongue, but no. The heart has stopped. The haze of insects flies overhead, and onwards. I surround the waiting flesh.

A pain. At the verge of tasting. A wet feeling in the round part of my body. All my concentration was focused on the frog. My defences were down. Just like the frog watching the insects, I am prey. Who? Who will I die for? I turn, in the few heartbeats I have remaining in this green home, and I see: myself. A black spider, the size of a human fist, with silken hairs on its legs. It looks at me without emotion. We have both spent our venom sacs, we are depleted. After feasting, the spider must hide and rest until its venom has been replenished. Beat-beat-beat. Perhaps three left. The frog will be delicious. My final thought? A foolish one. We could have shared the frog.

Francis

Four-thirty a.m.

Nine-thirty at night in London.

I start at the top of my head and observe my body. My entire scalp is itching. I identify the location of the itches one by one, systematically. I note the strength and nature of the itch. Burning, strong. Tickling, medium. Ant's legs, weak. I move down to my forehead and begin the analysis of my face, the two halves that I have established. The left nostril is dominant, the left side of my face feels larger, more active, brighter in colour. My left ear is throbbing. The right side of my face is quiet, weaker, pale, and the nostril is blocked.

I move down. My neck, my chest, my abdomen. My stomach creaks with a request for food, and I hear another stomach nearby responding. Soon, there are stomachs across the hall churning, squeaking, gurgling, moaning. Someone sneezes. Someone coughs. Several people are suppressing yawns. The coughing gets louder and the perpetrator stands and tiptoes down the rows of meditators to the door. Two hours until breakfast. I tell my stomach to quiet.

Refocus. Abdomen, legs, feet, toes. Moving the concentration over each part of the body in symmetry, as we have been told. Symmetrical observation. If dark thoughts rise, observe them and let them go. Keep moving the attention. Top of the neck, upper back, lower back, buttocks. The entire body observed.

Now again, faster. Everything is changed. The top of the head: tingling. The scalp: ant's feet itching. Nose: right nostril dominant. Right side of the face: now active and larger, subtle throbbing. Left side of the face: passive and cold.

Everything we see, hear, touch, smell, imagine, everything is vibrating *kalapas*, rising, rising, passing. My right nostril, my entire body, this meditation centre, the jungle, the sky, the ocean, the cities of the earth, our thoughts, our words, our breath: they are all just vibrating energy.

Everything is movement.

Everything is changing.

I am changing.

Anicca, anicca, rising and passing away.

I emerge in the early light from the meditation hall and turn towards the wooden pathway that winds along the edge of the jungle.

I am experiencing parallel paradigms. The first, the mindset I came here with: the heightened awareness of risk; the heartbreak of Jimme; the feeling that I am not safe anywhere; the sense of total vulnerability, that we – humans – are not safe anywhere; the terror of imminent attack.

Running parallel to this: an impression of my own fluidity, my own brief existence, a gathering of atoms that will rise and pass and there is nothing to do but accept it, for this is what it is, whether it is science saying it or spirituality saying it, this is what can be observed. I will pass, Jimme will pass, risks will come and some will be fulfilled and terrible things will take place, and then they too will pass. Old threats will pass, new threats will come and pass. Fears will be seen and then they too will pass.

Then what is the point of anything? Anything at all?

· · ·

My father puts down his wine glass and pushes a Gitane out of the packet. The sun is setting over the Provence farmhouse and the scent of grasses and lavender makes the air fragrant. The cicadas are humming in the background. Papa is about to make a speech and Maman and I have exchanged a look. We know how this will go.

"It's the Americans," Papa begins. This was the way he usually started his polemics. Sometimes he would wave a newspaper around or a book he was reading. Today, he was without props, but he knew the speech by heart. "They are making the entire world stupid. They bring their empty values to every country in the world and they present them shamelessly, as if big cars and money and wars are something to be proud of. And the whole world suffers. Pfaw!"

It was Papa's sound of disgust, and it was hard for Maman and me not to giggle when he made it. We often whispered the sound behind his back to make ourselves laugh when he was being particularly unbearable.

Papa's belief was that only the ancient civilisations had any merit, and that since the Egyptian, Persian, Greek and Syrian cultures had passed into ancient history, mankind had been on a cultural slide down to total ignorance. French culture – "if you can even call it culture" – was the best of the surviving civilisations, but he had a particular hatred for some. The Americans bore the brunt of this animosity, then the English with their terrible food and arrogance (Maman slams the plates of salami and cheese down on the table), the Germans... he could talk all night about the shallowness of each country's position, stubbing the Gitanes angrily into the ashtray and pouring the red wine (French, of course) into the glasses.

"But Papa!" I begin, looking worriedly at mother. She puts a hand on my shoulder.

"Don't worry, Francis," she whispers. "Your papa hasn't noticed I am English yet. It will be our little secret."

. . .

I fold my legs into the meditation pose.

I focus on this separation of self, this crack that is opening between the *me* who is lying heartbroken in a Shepperton ditch, watching the Martians thud and roll; and a *me* that expands and flows along with the waves of continual molecular transformation that are occurring... everywhere... and at all times.

And now, through this gap, I can see that the first state – the state of fear, of burnished emotion – is entirely false. That, scientifically, it has no meaning. The fear is not real. The emotions are not real. The hypothesis will not stand examination.

I delve into the crack, and widen.

And yet, while these thoughts are occurring, I am performing Vipassana, running the focus of my concentration over my symmetrical body, observing the change... observing the change... *anicca*... And yet, *the risks are real*, my mind screams.

Observe. Right leg: numb after just a few minutes seated cross-legged. Left leg: tingling in an intensely pleasurable way, yet one which promises to shift into a painful inability to move by the next sweep...

The risks are real. Attacks are being planned all over the planet, in every single country of the earth, at this very moment; attacks to kill, to destroy, on small scales, on huge scales, indiscriminate people, specific people. And the risks from *beyond*. The likelihood that our planet is the only one with intelligent lifeforms being exactly zero, and the fact that any intelligent lifeform would obviously disguise itself while approaching our belligerent, unstable, fear-infested, resource-stripped and half-mangled ball of green and blue before carrying out whatever carefully drawn-up operation they had decided upon... We would have no chance at all. My finest brain, my double first in natural sciences brain, tells me that at any given moment of any day, lifeforms from more developed planets and civilisations could arrive and carry out their effortless plans and we would all become slaves. Or die. Or be transported to another planet to allow Earth to recover and be their playground. But because we humans are so arrogant as to believe that if we are not able to perceive another civilisation then it can't possibly exist, despite the fact that knowledge transforms and inverts every few generations, and that we are the Thanksgiving turkey, we are the turkey feasting on rich grain and waddling around the farmyard, worrying about the state of our feathers, and when October comes, or December, then it is all over...

And we never imagined.

But I imagine.

I imagine.

Breathe.

Lean into the crack.

I think I have fallen into the crack.

Start again, Francis. Start again.

The top of my head is tingling.

Breathe.

The risks are not real, I tell my mind. The risks are constructed possibilities pieced together by a brain that has taken in too many images of disasters and potential catastrophes and is now experiencing an overload. What is real is the movement of atoms. What is real is the change. The Buddha figured this out. The Buddha is not wrong. I am wrong.

Mr Goenka says our minds spend their time divided between projecting the future and reminiscing in the past, neither of which in fact exist. Mr Goenka says we must learn to look with clear eyes at the present moment. Focusing on the sensations of our bodies holds us in the present moment.

I am sweeping my body symmetrically. Everything has changed. Now there is no tingling but a heaviness in all the limbs, as if they have grown ten times in mass and I would not be able to rise from the floor even if every drop of effort was poured into the action. I know this to be one of my body's warning signs, but I ignore it. No, I observe it. I continue. This is how it would feel if extra-terrestrial lifeforms were to seal our atmosphere and adjust the gravity level. It would take so little. From 9.8 to 19.6 metres per second squared. A simple doubling on the scale and humans would be squirming like worms in hot sun. Unable to feed or water ourselves. Unable to sustain the worldwide supply economy that keeps us all alive. Unable to return to subsistence farming for lack of land, knowledge and the energy to do so. Although at that level of increase, the earth's core would probably have collapsed in on itself, and we would all have been cooked alive by the heat.

The warning signs are all here. The sense of my limbs increasing in mass is growing stronger. I observe my thoughts skipping gaily outside the orbit of mental control. I know what is ahead.

It is such a simple way to rid a planet of an intelligent but aggressive species that is incapable of uniting to create a society beneficial to all, which is so utterly, utterly accessible. Overflowing resources, unlimited communications, medical solutions for ninety percent of the planet's illnesses… and yet… and yet we humans cling on to our individual buckets of privilege; we cling on to the riches of our countries; we refuse to look further, wider, beyond. And if we cannot do it for our one, single planet, if we cannot share the food, medicine and education that we have enough of, then why should a more advanced civilisation take pity on us? Why shouldn't we be destroyed and have our planet taken over by a species that will nurture it, and exist in a constructive and cooperative manner?

Now I am tumbling further into the crack. I return to the sci-fi book where a group of humans contacted extra-terrestrials to come and take over Earth, as they were so disillusioned with the inability of homo sapiens to do anything but create new forms of suffering.

Would I be in that group? Would I betray my own planet? Would it be preferable to send out a message into space and just wait, knowing that the worst was coming? Would that make it easier? Not having to wonder if and when these terrible things were going to take place, just being able to sink into the wave of relief knowing that the worst was coming and that it would soon be over...

But in that case, if things are so very bad, why should I play a part in destroying the entire planet? If things are so terrible, why not just remove myself from this unbearable waiting game?

The old panic is rising.

Observe: sweat forming on the forehead and extreme heat spreading over entire body.

Observe: back of the neck burning.

Observe: difficulty drawing breath into lungs. Oxygen intake reducing.

Observe: heartbeat elevated and increasing.

Observe: dizziness zigzagging through brain and body.

Observe: tear glands producing steady supply of lacrimal fluid which cascades down cheeks.

Observe: mind and body in state of terror and panic.

Observe: it was all for nothing.

Lying on my bed.

Tor is standing over me and staring with sympathetic eyes. He holds his fists clenched near to his heart to express solidarity. I nod my head so far as I can. I know how I look: face like washed chalk, hair wet with perspiration. Body limp and boneless. Eyes, tragic.

It's a sad sight. It's the reason Jimme won't be in the flat when I return. He couldn't bear my *episodes*, as he called them. He told me, in a rare moment of true openness, that he had seen too many crimes committed against gay men in his home country. Houses burned, beatings, killings. He just couldn't bear my self-inflicted pain. His people had to walk tall with memories of friends dead and cruelties that would break a man like me. And that was what it came down to. I wasn't strong enough for him. He wasn't willing to enter the space of my imagined fears and protect me. He was disgusted by the lack of self-control. By the pure indulgence of it.

It gave me a flash of the walls that he had constructed around himself, of how the radiance of his smile was a distraction, his happiness a barrier keeping others away from his experience of pain, from his true story.

I respect that, Jimme. You have the right to deal with your past in your own manner, especially if it is not hurting anyone else. Especially when it is expressed in such a gentle way, as your shifting screens of welcoming charm. And I think, now, Jimme, that it would be better if you were to be with someone from your own country, be it a woman or a man. There would be an unspoken understanding of the harshness by which you were both shaped; the hardships of life which must never be told; the importance of approaching each day with simple pleasure and gratitude.

So, goodbye, Jimme. My mind-terrors were too infantile for your palate. My European indulgences of thought were too innocent for the reality that you have lived. I respect that. Thank you, Jimme. I will not try to follow.

Breathe.

DAY NINE

Laeticia

JUAN.

Driving through Finland. A surprise trip for my birthday to see the Northern Lights.

Winter. Snow. White and grey. Grey and white. White and white.

"Stop the car," he said.

"Why?" I asked.

"Just pull it over," he said. "Let's do something."

I indicated into the slow lane and edged the car up onto the curb. He leant to the back seat and drew a red scarf out of his rucksack.

"Juan?"

He took my hand and kissed it, first the top, then the palm.

"Do you have something brightly coloured?" he asked.

"I've got an orange jumper," I said. "I've got a purple scarf."

"Can you get them and put them on? There's something we need to do."

I took off my black coat and put on the jumper from my suitcase in the trunk. I wrapped the purple scarf around my neck.

"Dance with me," he said.

The cars were whizzing through grey slush. The trees were coated with heavy snow. In the distance was white, white, white. The colour had been stripped out of the landscape. Juan was the colour.

He set a Latin love song on his phone and raised it to full volume. Then he slipped it into the top pocket of his jacket and we began to dance. Red and orange and purple. Two lovers swaying in the snow by the side of the road. He turned me, I swung round; he bent me back, I rose towards him; his arms were around me, I pulled away and returned.

We were the colour on the white landscape. Juan was the colour. It was in his gaze, his mind, his body. He brought the streak of laughter, because it was him. He brought the dawn sunlight because each day was new for him. He brought a child's delight to the world because it was his playground.

We danced. Red, purple and orange. The drivers passed – *hum, whiz, slosh* – tyres on wet roads, wheels on water, grey asphalt threading into endless white and grey. They saw us dancing and one car hooted, but they saw us and they saw that colour was possible in that bleak setting. They saw that happiness was a choice.

Thank you, Juan. Thank you for the colour. Thank you for the memory. Thank you for the lesson that every situation is what I bring to it. Thank you for passing through my life and splattering your paints around for a while. Thank you for sharing this short time. You have moved on. I let you go. I hold on to nothing.

Rapist. I cannot thank you. What you did was evil. But because of you I will never stop fighting for the women who have less choice than me. The women who lose not only possession of their bodies, but of their homes, their children, their minds. They are my family now, whereas before they were ideas, shadows of suffering. But now I am inside their circle, and I will fight for them always. Rapist, this is a gift to women. Because of your actions, I will take down you and everyone like you. With laughter and colour and rage flowing through me. Yes. And if I ever see you – I will hurt you. I will use my physical strength to attack you and cause you harm and you will know how it feels.

I apologise, Mr. S. N. Goenka, but sometimes peace is not enough to teach a lesson. My plan is purely altruistic. I will do it for the sake of his soul. For the sake of his personal growth and understanding. So, live in fear, rapist. Because I am walking the streets unafraid – and my body will remember you.

Mama. You spent your life serving father and ironing his shirts. I don't want Beatriz to know a woman's life can be spent like this. But you came from a different age and I don't know what your choices were. Forgive me, Mama. I will talk to you and I will listen. I will hear your story and I will understand why you could not be president or have someone bring you coffee in the morning, or a partner to iron your shirts.

Beatriz. You have my passion and intelligence. I will teach you how to strap on a helmet and ropes and climb any mountain you choose. What I will not teach you is my rage. It is my own and I will not pass it on to you. I demand everything from your life. You will be happy. Your career will be outstanding. You will have lovers who satisfy every desire. You will own your body and your home independently. You will own your car and your bank accounts will have your name on them. You do not need to get married. You can have as many or as few partners as you wish. Treat them well. Share the joy. Move on when you are ready. Beatriz, I will give you the gift of my happiness. This promise I make to myself. This promise I make to you.

And betrayal? I no longer feel it. I feel the pain from Juan leaving, but it is more like a toothache when the tooth has been removed, not the screaming agony while it is being pulled out. The ache will fade. The pain will merge into the general memory of forgotten suffering. Juan was true to himself. He walks among his slides and see-saws, diverted by new games, new ways to express his playfulness and desire for pleasure. Let it be. But now, I, on my mountain, have a set of paints and a brush. As I go, I will leave great swathes of colour, so that those following will know that I was here – that I climbed, that I laughed, that I was happy.

Each time I sweep my body, from the top of my head, down to my feet and up again, each time I search for sensations arising and passing, the thoughts arise, the images arise, a flash of memory, accompanied by a pain, an ache, a throbbing, a twitching, a pulsing, a shaking... and then I move on, and with the next sweep the sensation is the tiniest bit duller, the flash of memory more like the page of a book I once read and less like a live event replaying in my active mind.

I have reclaimed my truth. I have reclaimed myself. I have released the parts that were not me. I can be a mother. I can run my café. I can hear the story of my own mother. I know who my family is. I will eat oysters.

Breathe.

"My God, that hurt!"

"Show me again."

"Doesn't yours?"

Anabel lifted her sleeve and there it was: our mountain.

"It's gorgeous."

I looked down at my arm to check the identical image. Towering peaks. Inspiring heights. Reach, achieve, reach, achieve.

"I need a drink."

We slipped into a bar just down the street. It was self-consciously filthy, but then we were in the East Village and anything clean or glamorous started ten blocks north.

"Two double Scotches," Anabel declared as we took seats at the beer-slicked counter. "Hey," she continued to the bar tender, "we just got matching tattoos." We lifted our sleeves, Anabel's left and mine right, and the woman examined them.

"Neat," she said, and pushed the drinks over to us. "Mean anything special?"

"It's the mountains we've gotta climb every day," said Anabel, "just to be a woman in the world and make something of it. We wanted to remind ourselves that it's not only tough, it's worth it, and it's awesome at the top."

The bar server nodded. "I get that," she said and nodded again.

"It still hurt like hell–" I began, then caught sight of the woman's arms, which were inked from top to bottom. "Guess that's not news to you, huh?" I finished.

"You know what?" the server replied, "these drinks are on the house." She turned and poured a tumbler of Scotch for herself, and we clinked glasses. "Good luck with your mountains."

Breathe.

Ivan

The final day without speaking. Tomorrow, they will ask us to say some words.

I haven't missed it. There is nothing I want to say. I am feeling calmer and stronger every hour. I have not cried since Tuesday. My Adidas is clean. It is not covered in blood and tears. Even the mosquitos have stopped biting me.

The food – I still sit alone in the dining hall – is changing me too. I have great plates of the green vegetable curry they serve, with rice. Bowls of pineapple and mango and papaya, sweeter than I've ever tasted. My body looks forward to this food. Then it looks forward to the walk along the wooden balcony down to the path that winds in one direction towards the jungle, while the women walk the opposite way. I don't even miss the women. There was one, the tall one. So beautiful. But I have too much to sort through to even think about her. Zhenia. Katya. Myself. My monk. The spider.

I wonder if they would let me stay here if I asked them. I could help out. I could meditate and then sweep the paths or chop some fruit. I could stay until I was truly healed.

Here we go. It's the last day of silence.

. . .

Mr. S. N. Goenka: "Ivan, what do you truly need to heal from?"

My mother: "Ivanushka, what is wrong? What is hurting?"

Me: "My heart is hurting from all the mistakes I have made and all the ways I have betrayed and been betrayed."

My mother: "Ivanushka, you can ask God for forgiveness."

Me: "If I wanted that answer I'd have gone to a church. I'm here in a Thai jungle."

My mother: "God is everywhere, Vanya."

Me: "So is betrayal. So is the pain I carry. They hurt me, Mother. Zhenia tried to kill me by taking away what I loved."

My mother: "What did he take away?"

Me: "Our friendship. Our brotherhood."

My mother: "Brotherhood is not something you can take away. Eat this soup I've cooked you. I just bought the meat from the market. The bread is fresh too. I'm sure Zhenia's mother would tell him the same. Ask forgiveness from God and then apologise to Zhenia."

Me: "What do you think, Mr. S. N. Goenka?"

Mr. S. N. Goenka: "I think it is time to meet God, Ivan."

Me: "How do I meet him?"

Mr. S. N. Goenka: "Your monk will take you there."

My mother: "Vanya! Your soup will go cold!"

My monk is holding out his hand. His face is glowing. He must have done an overnight avocado mask. I have never held a man's hand. I put mine into his and it feels like sparkling water, his fingers like tubes of light. Not physical. Perhaps he is not physical at all. The monk I pushed in the dining room was. He had a backside to fall on. Never mind. It's not a physical feeling, is what I'm saying, and by holding my hand in his, my hand and arm and then my entire body feel less physical and more like tubes of light. It's easier to walk. It takes less effort – we're more or less floating. My legs are doing the actions, but there's very little effort needed.

My monk doesn't speak. He leads me to a door. The door is green. He lets go of my hand and motions towards it.

"Will you come with me?" I ask, with gestures.

"If you want me to," he replies with his eyes.

I nod.

I open the door.

Inside is a humming jungle.

I don't see the walls of the room because the jungle is thick. I step in, finding a foot-space between tree ropes and low plants that could have deadly animals beneath them. The monk enters after me. It's easier than it might have been, with our lighter bodies. The monk closes the door behind us. It is green on the inside, too.

So, God is in here?

I step through the plants and among the tree trunks, finding footholds on the leafed soil. Now that the door is closed, the noise is getting louder, a humming and hissing that is made from invisible animals and plants, and it seems even the air is buzzing, perhaps water is running and dripping – everything in this jungle room is making a noise and the noise is one noise. The jungle is singing. A screech, a frog-laugh, an answering cackle, a close-by hiss. And then I see the movement. I had thought that I was walking through a still landscape, but now I see a leaf twitching and a grass bending and a rope swinging and a beetle opening its wings and a tongue flickering and air heavy with water and below me a floor of barely visible micro-creatures transforming the ground into waves of rolling patchwork. Everything is moving. Everything is singing. Then I notice that I, too, am singing. I am giving out a low hum, providing the bassline of the song, and I look at my limbs and see that I, too, am in motion. I see my atoms dancing in the light tubes. I see the blood gurgling through my veins. I see cells tumbling off my skin and new ones appearing. I see the oxygen rushing around my body and my heart churning to the beat of my deep hum. It's all happening.

My monk gestures forward. We walk, and it's easier now, because my body is in constant, dancing motion and everything else is in constant, dancing motion, but my heart is providing the beat and my humming is setting the key and the jungle moves and sings and curves as we walk, leaf-hidden insects swaying from foot trajectories, branches bending towards outstretched hands.

We go forward until we arrive at a clearing. There is a natural platform here made from a flat, smooth tree trunk, and my monk gestures to me to sit.

I take up my meditation pose, with crossed legs. Everything is still moving and singing around me. I lay a hand on each knee and put my forefinger and thumb together, as I've seen the meditators do in the hall. My monk nods, then he crouches down in front of me and smiles. The light of his smile fills my face and fills the tubes of my limbs with tingling happiness. Now I'm smiling. He keeps smiling and I keep smiling and I suddenly wonder with a quick fear if he's going to kiss me, and then I blink my eyes open and then closed and he's gone. But it's part of the plan. So, I keep smiling and I just listen to the music and resume my humming and feel the cells of my body growing and falling from me and feel the blood travelling around my organs and feel the thoughts being processed in my brain and feel all the thoughts of the jungle being processed through the green brain-canopy above and the occasional threads of sunshine flashing through seem like revelations from this great, green mind.

Then I go higher and feel the organs and limbs of the galaxy stretching in their own body, their shape and logic clearer the further I go, and ruled by their own intelligence. Higher still, from structure to structure to mind to larger body and looking down I see it all as a sea of tiny bodies, not unlike the sea of insects rustling beneath the leaves here in the jungle, rustling, bent with utter intensity on their tasks, the bearing of a corpse to feed their clan; the building of a home to lay their eggs; the preening of black casing to win their mate.

Pattern on pattern. Layer on layer. Lifeform on lifeform. System on system. Song on song. I go up. I go higher. The song quietens. The movement condenses. It slows. It shrinks into a smaller space. The light tubes of my limbs shrink, my emotions intensify, I am happier now. The monk's smile and my smile are smiling together. All the happiness is feeding back into my heart. All the singing and all the humming and all the laughing and the flickering and the rustling and the squawking, they are all pushing back, back, back into my heart and the happiness is urgent now, it's intense and urgent and I think, *this is the most fantastic feeling ever! This is what a heart attack must feel like!*

And then my heart explodes.

Black. Black. Black. Laughter. Green. Happiness. Song. Jungle.

"Mother," I say. "I'd like that soup now, please."

Francis

Four-thirty a.m.

Nine-thirty at night in London.

I will try again.

An image of my mother. My bedroom in the Paris apartment. She is stroking my head.

"It's alright, Francis," she is saying. "It's alright. The stories are not real."

The borders of the memory don't include what images were fizzing in my brain at that moment, or how my mother had noticed my distress. The memory is very simple. Her seated form. Her hair brushed, long and yellow. Her soft hand moving over my forehead. Relief.

I will try again.

I do not have to go back to the same job. There are wildly overpaid jobs for scientists all over the world. I could do any of those. I could dedicate myself to humanitarian causes, searching for a cure, distributing vaccines. I think the latter one would lead me back to this place. I would become tortured by the suffering I was not able to reach. But something must change.

Looking around the hall, I see Tor a few rows ahead. His pose is erect and his concentration evident. He is absorbed in the Vipassana process. He is freeing himself from the false realities of the external world. He is experiencing truth by observing it directly: that everything changes, constantly.

I check on the cloaked figure, but he is motionless. I glance surreptitiously round to monitor the familiar meditators. The Thai men around me, who I recognise more from their physical shapes than their faces. The man beside me with the child's body; another, muscular, with heavy shoulders and neck. One tall with a body slack and untoned. Then the sobbing giant, the earnest Canadian, the fidgeter and, across the line, the tall woman rising over the others with grace and serenity, beside her a foreigner with messy blonde hair; the sound of breath, the turning fan, the heaviness of concentration.

It came to me last night, as I was drifting off, the jungle rustling through my open window, my body weak from the panic attack, that everyone here is seeking a peaceful solution to the disorder of their souls. Even if it's a mild disorder. Even if they're simply overwhelmed by technology and information. Or overwhelmed with the heaviness of being alive. I felt a great empathy, lying in bed and listening to the jungle, for all the people who had come here looking for peace, as I have come, now, to this place, in paranoia, heart-pain and fear, looking for the world to reassure me of its inherent goodness, looking for some lighter feeling that I could expand, nurture, recreate through my darkness.

The empathy turned to something stronger and the warmth was rising out of me faster than I could contain it until I was weeping. I wanted to go outside to the room next to mine and knock on the door. It's the Canadian's, the one with the toe rings, and I wanted to take him in my arms in a gesture of unified brokenness and say, "I am terrified that I will never feel safe again. I am terrified that I will always feel divided between two states and not be able to commit my full self to anything. I am terrified that because of this I will be alone and scared, always."

In my imagination, the Canadian allowed me to speak the

words. He listened calmly and then he said: "I am here to achieve enlightenment. I am leaving behind the burdens of this world to follow the path of Dhamma. After this I will spend ninety days in silence and give all my worldly goods to charitable causes."

"Thanks for listening," I said, horribly embarrassed. I struggled out of the embrace and found that we were entangled with our arms and hair and fingers, and for a few moments our faces were lip to lip as we wrestled to get the loose strands of his man-bun away from the button on my sleeve. I felt the love seeping out into uncomfortable tension as we unwound tendrils of his hair. It wasn't too clean. His lips, almost meeting mine, were puffy and moist.

There. We had disentangled from one another. Time to go. "Thanks for listening," I said again. "We shouldn't really be talking. I just had this love surge and wanted to come and share it." Is that what guys say? Is that *guy speak*? Or is that international-gender-fluid yoga-love language? I don't know anymore. I just don't want those puffy lips so close to me again.

"You're welcome anytime," he said.

Or I imagine he might have said.

And then I started psychoanalysing the incident I'd imagined. Me offering my broken self, assuming everyone else is broken, and discovering that no, in fact, I'm the only one broken. Everyone else is fine. Everyone else is leaping ahead on the enlightenment ladder, having solved their major life problems years ago. I was the only one whose nerves were frazzled from fear. And the moment I opened up I was shamed and rejected, not in a bad way, but in a subtly embarrassing way. *Everyone else has moved on, buddy. No worries, we'll help you get there. We've all been where you are – years and years ago.*

· · ·

Lunchtime. A pile of stewed vegetables and a walk on the path next to the building, gazing out at the jungle. It feels a little like a prison here. Enforced routine. Strict limits on food, exercise and possessions. Constant monitoring. I have a small panic on the boardwalk. What if I start to run towards the jungle and the monks run after me? What if they shut me in my room and keep me meditating until they are satisfied I've reached enlightenment? What if it all becomes a dystopian monkmare of cold-eyed captors and forced silence?

The ninth day is not going well. My mind is jumping all over the place. It is as if, at the first sign of progress, at the first hint of breaking through into a realm of honesty and communion, my mind has transformed from its normal state of chattering monkey into a vicious, hundred-foot ape, picking up the pieces of potential joy and smashing them down. My head is hurting. Not a headache, but as if the ape has taken all the fragile constructions of hope and future and smashed them physically inside my skull. Hurting. Pain.

In the evening, we watch our prescribed video. The honourable Mr. S. N. Goenka. He sits cross-legged, adorned in a simple white robe. His voice is monotonous and steady. His eyes are calm and sure. We sit, and his words ring out through speakers around the huge room. He tells us how we must continue our meditation practise when the course is finished and continue the study of our internal worlds. He tells us how we should live: a proper life, a moral life, a peaceful life. Good for oneself and good for others.

Thank you, Mr. S. N. Goenka. But I tried that.

My job was to save the world from future threats, and it resulted in my own mind attacking itself. Now I'm here. But I won't give up. I'll try something new, Mr. Goenka. I'll work to find cures for diseases, I'll volunteer at a women's refuge, I'll join Médecins Sans Frontières and serve tirelessly with them. I'll give blood every week. I promise you, Mr Goenka, that I will leave behind these distorted dualities that twist any sense of unity. I will find a simple path ahead, something good for me and good for others.

Breathe.

DAY TEN

Laeticia

THE FIRST MEDITATION session of the final day.

Good morning!

My face in the small mirror: peaceful. What a wonderful cliché. My eyes in the small mirror: shining. Another cliché. My body as I step onto the balcony and stretch: willing, open.

Am I enlightened, Mr. Buddha? Am I closer? Did *you* have to check in the mirror to see if your eyes were shining? Possibly not.

One thing I am sure of: I am healed. I am in the present. The sleeping volcanoes can throw up lava, but it will turn to ash and blow away in the wind of my happiness. It will dissolve in the fulness of my fulfilment.

This evening we will start to speak again. But first, the

meditation: Mettā, the practice of loving kindness. I am so used to sitting still, it will be strange not to assume this position, on the floor, for eleven hours a day. I wonder how I will adjust back to the world. Will it take a week? A month? My flight to Rio is tomorrow evening. I will be able to hold Beatriz again. On the journey I will write to my mother and say that I want to know more about her life and her stories. I will write to Anabel and tell her that we did it, she and I. With our hard work and determination. We did it.

But today, the final day, will be for pleasure. I am calm. I am happy. Now, I will enjoy the peace, knowing that tomorrow I return to the furious bustle of the world. The cities, the dramas, the hurricane of words, the responsibilities of other people's lives. Today: my own. Today: the quiet in myself and the quiet of the figures around me.

I have felt a change within my body. Not the release of rage and hurt. Not the shifting of perception to a place of understanding where I can empathise with all of humanity. A change in my physical self – the parts that were closed, the limbs that betrayed me when I was in direst need, the eyes that saw a face lit up by the Paris streetlights. It must have been the meditation, the Vipassana, observing over and over again that everything is in constant movement, that our cells are renewing in every moment, for the physical form that walked the steps of the meditation centre ten days ago is not the same one I now occupy. Everything has transformed. And that has brought peace.

From the place that was closed has arisen a sense of great anticipation. As my body has opened, so too has the world. I look ahead and begin to plan. I sense ideas trembling on the periphery of my desire. But wait. There is time. I will reach in to catch them. But there is time.

This new lightness I sense not only in myself. The women sitting in front of me, their shapes are relaxed. I observe the tension has gone. The women sitting on each side of me are breathing deeply. At breakfast there were smiles, there was light in the eyes of the meditators. People took little food. *We are here,* the eyes seemed to say; *we have achieved what we came for; today we will celebrate; today is the most precious time, the achievement of peace, the knowledge of the approaching world, the height of our happiness.* Will any of us in this room ever achieve such a level of serenity again? In our entire lives, as we dive back into the storm, we will have great highs and lows, but will we ever again feel this calm, so intensified by the knowledge that tomorrow it will end?

What words would I speak now?

None.

What thoughts would I have now?

Those of loving kindness.

What people would I see now?

Those infused with goodwill.

Lunch. A cup of tea. A walk. And then the final Mettā meditation, sending love to all beings everywhere. And then speech.

This is it. The final hours. This time tomorrow I will be on a bus. This time tomorrow the magic will be broken. My sanctuary will be gone.

I will miss hearing the sound of the jungle. The night-time laugh of frogs; the constant hum and rustle; the knowledge of this unstoppable entity so close by, this body of life that could destroy me, something within which I am vulnerable. It is so very humbling. Just a few steps away is a world that is not my own. I, human, do not control everything.

I will miss the words of Mr. S. N. Goenka. I will miss having people around me who are seeking something higher. I will miss the simple clothes. I will miss the warm air that makes us feel like animals, that we could be naked and our bodies could adjust back to survival, away from the insanity of our constructed luxury. I will miss the sharpening of my senses: my hearing – the feet of monkeys on the roof, the hornbill screech; my touch – feeling the cells of my skin transforming; my smell – ripe papaya and thick rain; my sight – viewing my surroundings with clarity and love.

And what will I return to? My desires are rising again, and this time I allow them. Images are flashing into my mind. A new apartment. A different *arrondissement*. White walls, decorated by my own hand. Overalls covered with streaks of eggshell, ivory and lace. Brushes and rollers. A cream panelling. Windows flooding light into a room of bright paint and tall, green plants.

Yes.

Beatriz. Reading, reading, reading. Reading French, Portuguese, English. Laughing and dancing. Watering the plants with a small watering can. Hair tied with a white ribbon. Hair tied with a blue ribbon.

And me. Standing in the sunshine that floods through the windows. A background of white and green. Loose, natural clothes. A body peaceful and renewing, constantly renewing.

Me. Sitting in the centre of the white room, surrounded by tall, green plants. Contemplating choices. Laughing. So many wonderful choices. Which order to start lining them up into action? Which order to choose what to bring to the lip of reality? I will not rush! I will sit some more! I will laugh some more!

I will choose.

Yes.

Yes.

Yes.

I am ready.

The teacher: "Turn now in pairs to one another. Take your

partner's hands in your own. Feel their energy. Look into their eyes. Smile. Think of one word you choose to be your first word after our days of silence. When you are ready, speak that word. It will be a word that you remember. You may repeat it several times."

My partner is Thai. She has long black hair and a loose orange T-shirt. She smells of almonds. She takes my hands and holds them between her own. Her eyes are dark brown, without flecks. She will speak first.

"Peace," she says. Her voice comes out deep and cracked. She clears her throat and licks her lips. She looks pleased with herself. I manage not to laugh. It is too obvious. I never liked obvious.

She looks at me expectantly. I switch our hands around so that I am now holding hers. They are small and hot; the palms a little damp.

I know my word.

We look into each other's eyes.

I am ready.

I clear my throat. I lick my lips. I run my tongue around the inside of my mouth.

I am ready.

She smiles at me.

"Sim," I say. My voice does not croak. It is clear. She does not know the word. I smile. "Sim," I say again. My word is quiet, it is powerful. I translate it for her: "Yes."

Ivan

The final day of meditation.

I put on my last, brand-new white Adidas suit. Long silky trousers. Clean T-shirt. Zip up the top.

I stopped shaving when I came here and my stubble has grown into a beard. They took away the gel for my hair so it is long and flops over my head. They took away my aftershave so I smell of soap and clean clothes.

My eyes looking out of this hairy, soft face are different. They came angry, raging, agonised, desperate, lost. Now they are calm, questioning, thoughtful, challenging, hopeful.

Without anyone telling me: I breathe.

The final day, and at the end we speak.

The final four a.m. gong.

I have not drunk vodka for ten days. I have not eaten meat for ten days. I have not been with a woman for ten days.

I don't feel hunted any more. Not by business partners. Not by people I have cheated or stolen from. Not by the desires and needs of my body. Not by my wife, children or lovers.

I feel calm in my body, whole, peaceful, centred. I feel my own power. I feel myself.

I am ready.

.   .   .

I sit at the back of the meditation hall. Orange-robed monks to the side. White line up the middle. Teachers on the platform at the front. Men on the left, women on the right. I have not paid much attention to the faces, but I look now. What transformations have they gone through? Two hundred people I estimate in the room. Have each of them seen God? Has Mr. S. N. Goenka been taking each of them on an individual journey? Have they all got a personal monk?

I see the tall girl on the edge of the women's section. Her head rises high over the others. I'll talk to her when we are permitted to speak. Perhaps if I had a lover who meditated then we would live together and be peaceful and rich. We could split our time between Thailand and Kyiv and eat green curry and make love in a big, lazy house made out of wood.

I could leave Eva in Kyiv with the children and come and stay here. I'd have no more stress. My days of hunting and slashing and cutting would be done. I'd start a local business. I'd import fruit to Ukraine. The tall girl would want me day and night. We'd roll in a huge, white bed and then eat more fruit and curry.

But the questions still remain.

I've left behind the anger and hurt. I've looked my love of Katya in the eye. My monk has returned my torn heart.

What to do now with Zhenia? What to do about the business? What to do about money?

If I don't have money in Kyiv, then I'll be nobody. Zhenia will be cruising around in his chauffeured Maybach, getting richer from my former company, gaining influence and power. I'll be the story behind it. *He stabbed his childhood friend in the back and took all his shares.* Nobody will trust their childhood friends anymore. They'll all be re-writing contracts and double-checking agreements. They'll be watching their wives more closely.

There are several scenarios.

Scenario One: Zhenia will refuse to see me. He has made his decision and will not let me near him ever again. His sneaky face will be surrounded by people who will never truly know him. Apart from Katya.

Observe reaction: Pain, panic, old feelings, desire to weep, sensation of mosquitos biting skin.

Scenario Two: He will happily see me. He will be waiting for me to come and apologise for sleeping with Katya. He will make it clear what the price of that is for me, and then we will come to a financial arrangement and continue our work together. I will take a massive hit on my companies and shares, but I'll be able to build up the business again.

Observe reaction: Shame, fear, pain, desire to destroy, mosquitos biting skin.

Scenario Three: I will return to find he has taken the revenge further. Eva and the children will be staying with her mother in their Kyiv flat, the house will have been taken over by a police investigation. All passports confiscated.

Observe reaction: Anger, determination, need to destroy, mosquitos.

Scenario Four: I will be arrested at Kyiv airport and thrown into jail. Add to that Scenario Three and Scenario One.

Observe reaction: Anger at self for stupidity and lack of preparation, mosquitos.

There. I have learned something. I have learned the gap from event to reaction. I have learned to pause and look at what is produced in between and then choose from it.

Plenty of feelings here. Mr. S. N. Goenka? What do I do with these feelings?

Mr. S. N. Goenka: "Ivan, the feelings are natural. Everyone has feelings. You do not have to act on any of them. Before you make a decision, examine your heart and your mind and follow your choice through a few steps."

Very well. Clear out the rage, pain, fear. Go beyond.

Tomorrow, I will call Eva. We will talk. I will call her from the car on the drive to Bangkok. She will tell me if Scenario Three is happening. Then I will call my lawyer. He will tell me if Scenario Four is happening. If it is looking bad then perhaps Eva should fly out to Thailand with the children? We could spend some months here and talk everything through. Maybe she wants to live abroad?

Although, maybe she has betrayed me too, by this time? Maybe she has taken a rich lover who will protect her. I doubt it. There are enough beautiful, single women for a rich man in Ukraine. He does not need one with a husband and children. She doesn't have the right instinct either. She wouldn't survive in a sinking ship. She's an accessory, not a fighter.

So, there we have it. It is one of these scenarios. But I have won the first battle. I am not dead. My heart has not stopped. Instead of dying, I have gained a belt full of weapons to keep my blood pressure down and I have tasted true happiness and met God. I have got myself a personal monk and a spiritual teacher. All this will remain secret. But after the first blow, I am not yet dead. *Shshe ne vmerla.* Just like Ukraine.

Tomorrow: call Eva. Call lawyer. Take next step. If I have to live in Thailand the rest of my life, I am ready. If the worst scenario is true, I am ready. There will be pain, some of it terrible. But I will prevail. I will call my mother. I will bring her to Thailand if need be.

Breathe.

One word, they said. You will say one word to the student sitting beside you. Think hard about the word you choose for it will set the tone of your path from the end of this course. The word should resonate with the path of Dhamma and the truth you choose to live.

Words that now mean something to me: God. Monk. Jungle. Spider. Mr. S. N. Goenka. Avocado. Breath. Pause. Gap.

Breathe.

It's time.

The person next to me is a small, Thai man in a pink T-shirt. We do the bowing-praying thing. He will go first. He licks his lips.

"*Whon kiin,*" he says. His voice is croaky. I don't know this phrase. He says it again, with slow nodding and reverence. "*Whon kiin.*" Then he says it in English: "Return."

I nod. It's a good word.

It's my turn. He's looking at me. All the wrong words are in my head now. Forgiveness. Truth. Love.

Mr. S. N. Goenka is before me. "I have a present for you, Ivan," he says. "It is something to take with you from here. It is for you to remember the path that we have walked together, the path to truth."

He hands something to me. It is a mirror. I look into it and there is the face of my orange monk. Shining avocado skin. Eyes that are fresh-water calm. A smile from the depths of a hurricane heart.

Yes. Yes. I understand! But I must say my word. I am desperate to say it now. I'm confusing languages. It's coming out in Russian.

"Mish…" I say. "Rrrrrrr," I say, rolling the 'r's. I try again. "Mish, mish, mish. Shen, shen, shen, I. I. I. E. E. E. Rrrrrrr," I say. The Thai man is trying to stay with me, but he's looking scared. He's remembering I'm the one they had to drag out of the dining room. I can do this. Give him the lake eyes. Give him the hurricane smile. "Mish… shen…"

The avocado face is pulling me back. Orange robe. Brothers around me. The reflection of mountains in clear water.

"Mish…"

The feeling in my gut is dragging me the other way. The neural pathways are activating. The pain of a kicked shin in childhood. A whipping from my mother. Stealing sandwiches because I was hungry. Chopping firewood for a cold house. Pain. Shame. Violence.

A calm lake!

A storm!

A sudden noise is building in me, a growl, more visceral than I have known before. A roar! I pick up my monk and release this fury upon him.

"I was made from pain and violence," my roar bellows into him. "It is all I have ever known. It is what I am."

My monk: "But I have shown you…"

Me: "Roar!"

My monk: "Please don't forget me…"

From the deepest notes of the vibration, my brain seeks the pleasure canals it knows will satisfy this pain and rage. A bubbling Jacuzzi full of strippers. A private jet with an endless supply of beluga. Silk sheets on the bed in my mansion, also with strippers. Riches on riches to dull the pain and memories. Here is my word. It's ready now. I can say it.

"Mish-en-i-e." I annunciate it clearly. "Mishenie."

The man still doesn't understand. I translate it for him.

"Revenge."

Francis

My face in the mirror. I drag my eyes up to meet their reflection.

I know the word I will speak.

Whole.

Two eyes, two ears, two arms, two legs, two names, two nationalities, two languages. Two states of being: reality and possibility.

It is time to end this.

Everything has led to this morning, to these minutes in the small bathroom. The jungle is humming and vibrating in a muted green light.

And now.

Four-thirty a.m.

In Thailand.

In a jungle.

In a meditation centre.

In a wooden hall.

On a blue mat.

Here.

Now.

Four-thirty a.m.

I am present.

I begin the Vipassana.

I focus my attention on each part of my body. I start with the top of my head (tingling wildly), and I move down symmetrically, covering each side of my form: neck, chest, arms, hands, trunk, hips, legs, feet.

And again.

As I do so, I create a circle around me made up of my word, *wholeness*. I weave this into a protective sphere and I increase my awareness of myself within this space. I am whole. I am protected in my wholeness. I will not divide, I will not fall apart, I will not shatter into fragments.

Breathe.

We are meant to be practising sending love and kindness to each other in today's meditation, but this is more important. I feel an urgent need to establish this state of wholeness in myself. I feel that now, after ten days of silence, it is possible.

As I sweep my concentration over my form, I seek all the experiences of my life and I welcome them into this space. I am seeking to unify. I am seeking to gather the fragments that have fallen into cobwebbed corners and beneath dusty sofas and bring them back into myself. Nothing rejected. Nothing broken. One, single self.

I collect the childhood memories: Paris, Provence, Papa, Maman, reading in French, reading in English; then schools, me in polished shoes and shorts, and then boarding school, running in cold, wet fields, boys everywhere, learning by rote, the science lab.

University: thrilling brains to talk to and interact with; women and sex, pints of beer, professors and wild, wonderful theories. Work that I loved doing, conversations I loved having. I bring these memories joyfully into the sphere.

Then the meeting in the pub, the job in Paris. A flat of my own. Men and sex, women and sex, restaurants, wine, independence.

And London. Jimme, Brixton, Hartbridge Laboratories, Leila

Massey; too much intensity, too much fragmentation, and I see, as I draw the shards into my circle, that this was where I broke, that Jimme's rejection of himself, and therefore of me, and the firework lit by Leila Massey and released into the caverns of my imagination, and the real work we were doing to prevent risks and attacks... this is where the balance, which had been rolling from side to side but just holding, tipped over, and I fell... I gather all these memories and I welcome them into the sphere, because I am determined to be whole.

I have them all. I hold them. I compress them.

This is me, I mouth to myself.

With this wholeness, I perform the Vipassana. I concentrate on the changes that I observe in each part of my body, on every new sweep. Tingling, aching, itching, throbbing, vibrating, flowing, allowing, preparing. I hold this wholeness of myself and I allow the concept of change to move through it. I am whole, I am whole, and yet I am constantly transforming.

All is well. All is good.

Breathe.

It is time.

Ten days of silence and now we will release the protection of our sanctuary.

A single word. Considered, held in peace, spoken with love.

I am partnered with the child-man. We are a foot apart. His body is even smaller than I had thought, his arms as thin as grass snakes. I try to imagine what his word will be. Will I be able to trace his entire path from this word, draw his life in desires and failures? What will he be able to tell about me?

I take his hands and speak first. I clear my throat and moisten my lips, unsure of the sound that will emerge.

I croak.

"Whole." A bark-scrape fading to nothing. I repeat it and it is louder. "Wholeness."

I say it once more, clearly now. "Whole."

The word embraces me with sudden, intense joy. I don't cry. I don't laugh. I close my eyes as my body is imbued with a flow of liquid happiness, from my feet, through my legs, my genitals, my torso, my chest and heart, my head, and down my arms to my hands.

I am whole. I am protected within my sphere.

Yes.

I am whole.

I open my eyes, aware that I must make a space for the child-man. He looks a bit impatient with my transcendence. I'm still flying. I nod at him, my eyes focused on his. We both know I have stolen the glory. But he's got to do it.

We switch the position of our hands.

"BMW," he says.

His eyes are on mine, nodding.

I tilt my head. Did I hear him correctly?

"B. M. W.," he repeats.

Now it is his turn to fly.

His eyes close and a film of delight washes over his body, and I get to watch from the outside what I have experienced from within. His face is smiling brighter and tighter and is widening, his entire body is shining, a light is pouring out from it; his wrinkled face is taking on ecstatic vestiges of beauty. He is, literally, bathed in light. From behind this miracle, I lever my conscious brain into logical thought. How much money do I have? Can I buy this man a BMW? I've got some savings. I don't see why not. I could probably buy him a 7 Series.

My joy in this thought amplifies the situation and now I'm sharing his transcendence. I'm going to get him his dream! I'm going to make it happen tomorrow! At the dealer in Bangkok!

He'll be cruising around, picking up yoga-women, making love to them on the backseat with his child body.

I can't tell how long the feeling continues. It's more intense than any orgasm I've experienced, the build-up and mindless wild push and fire of the climax. But this is like the pre-climax, combined with the release, and a little of the after-glow, all rolled into one and rolling, rolling in waves of pleasure: my pleasure, his pleasure, our pleasure. And he has no idea I'm going to buy him his car! This gives me more pleasure, which sets off new waves. I don't even know where my body is right now, it could be perched on a treetop in the jungle, it could be riding a wave in the Atlantic ocean, it could be that I've had a heart attack and died and this is what will be from now until evermore.

"Ksssss."

Bring it down.

"Kssss."

Open the eyes.

"Kssssss."

The child-man is looking at me. Clearly, his flight of joy has passed. My face must be a filthy mask of bliss. I can't help it. I can't change it.

I want to pick the child-man up and put him on my knee and embrace him. I want to whisper in his tiny ear that everything will be alright from now, that I will buy him his BMW, a 7 Series, black, with tinted windows and pimped wheels. I want to whisper to him that he will get all the yoga-women he has dreamed of. I want to whisper that he did right coming here, on this meditation course, that Mr. S. N. Goenka delivers. I want to whisper that everything will be good, starting from now.

I hold his hands in mine. Delicate, tiny hands. I resist stroking them. Soft, sunset skin.

Whole.

DAY ELEVEN

Laeticia

"YES."

I speak to the mirror and my eyes speak back to me.

Four-thirty a.m. There is no more meditation. There is no more silence.

We must leave by seven, and we must clean our rooms by then.

But I want the last minutes of quiet, and jungle.

I dress in a belted cardigan and sandals and go out into the hallway to the main balcony overlooking the dense mass of trees, which runs beside the canteen. This is the beginning of the approved walking area, right for women, left for men. The early light is grey, and the canopy has a covering of green-grey over it, like a mist. Like an exhaled breath. Normally, at this time, we are in meditation in the great hall. Wooden floor, blue cushions, a hundred exhalations. My body has slipped automatically into a semi-meditative state. It is breathing with the body of trees. Peace. Peace. I hear the rustle of the forest, the single mass of life stretched before me. I listen. I hear a distant shriek; something has been caught. I hear a bird chip-chipping and the tap of feet on the roof. I hear footsteps.

I turn. It is one of the men. He stops in the doorway of the canteen. He has come the same way as me. Our eyes meet. He is not sure whether to continue. I smile and hold out my hand. I think about the words I want to use. The power behind them.

"Welcome," I say.

He steps out on to the balcony and leans over towards the jungle, taking deep breaths.

"Wow," he says.

"I want to meditate," I say.

"I think I still am meditating," he says. He touches his head and then gestures towards the dense foliage.

"What was your word?" I ask. "What word did you say yesterday?"

Our eyes meet again.

"Wholeness," he says.

I let out a short laugh. "Appropriate!" I say.

He nods.

We look out again over the jungle. There are threads of orange permeating the grey. A rising pink. The light appears to be a living organism, humming, shifting, awakening. My body is alive to it. The silence and meditation have broken down a barrier that was between me and the rest of the world. I am responding. I am not exactly a part of these living organisms, but I am reacting to them naturally – as a living organism myself.

My body feels alive, alert, happy. It feels ready, poised,

excited. It wants to run; it wants to climb a tendril. It wants to… I turn towards the man.

His eyes are reflecting my own. *Choose!* My mind tells me. *Choose words. Choose actions.*

Yes, I say to myself. *Yes. This is a new choice. This is the beginning of the new. This is the new beginning. Happiness. Fun. Oysters. Dancing. Anaïs Nin.*

I think all this very quickly.

We move together naturally, as if no one had moved at all. We are kissing. Dry, careful, erotic, and then our arms are wrapped around each other and we are kissing; wet, exploring, jungle. My body is acting on its own, or the jungle is acting through my body, or it is an extension of the meditation, but there is no time for my body to shout, *Yes! Yes! Yes!* because it is happening, we are happening, right now, in the four o'clock meditation hour, I'm wearing nothing under my cardigan, he's wearing only shorts and we're making love, we're mating, we're meditating jointly with our bodies – no white lines here – against the barrier, the jungle is present, it's breathing, it's heaving, it's waking, it's humming, it's thrashing, it's singing, it's rising to meet the dawn, flowers opening, snakes lifting deadly heads, uncoiling, climbing, climbing. Oh! He's clinging to me. We're covered in sweat. The dawn has come. The jungle is open. A door is clanging. The breakfast staff. We separate. I'm tying my robe. He's steadying his breath. We're standing, side by side now, our bodies touching, breathing deeply, deeply. He reaches for my hand and intertwines our fingers.

My body is singing.

Yes, yes, yes, it is singing. *What a start. What a new start. What a choice. Happy, happy, happy.*

Ssshhhhh, I whisper to my body. *Sshhhhhhh,* I whisper. *The silence is enough.*

· · ·

Room cleaned. Bag arranged. Bus to Bangkok airport arriving in thirty minutes. I wait in the reception hall. The administrators will check my room and clear me to depart. In a few hours there will be new students arriving, dirty from airplanes and buses, minds teeming with drama, chaos and exhaustion, longing for relief. I picture them arriving in a thick dust of oppression, and each day, in that white hall, the dust rising from their minds and bodies. Heavy the first day, heavy the second day, and then lighter and lighter. And perhaps on the final day, a different mist, a faint gold or green rising, at last a substance that will feed back into the ether, beneficial, nourishing, organic. Something we could carry with us always and in any place that we might be, this lovely green organic living dust that would spread through any place and fill it with beneficence, with natural goodness. I picture my café, filled with green-gold dust. It is hovering on the air, cognisant, nurturing. Alive, poised, ready.

"Ms. Montes?"

"Yes."

"We've checked your room. You are free to go."

The entrance hall is crowded with people, women on one side, men on the other. I will wait for my bus outside.

I make my way to the porch and then step out onto the wide, wooden steps that lead down to the road. At the bottom of the steps, people are getting into buses and taxis. It's only seven o'clock but the heat is already heavy.

"Hello."

The tall man has approached me. He is holding out a large hand. He is unshaven and about twice the size of me.

Choose! Choose! my body says.

I do not want to touch him.

I open my hands into a greeting gesture and smile.

"Hello," I say.

He pulls his hand back and stands, nodding. He does not look pleased.

"Ivan," he says. "I saw you," he says.

"Yes," I reply. "You are very tall."

He smells of cigarette smoke and new clothes. It is not a smell from here – from the surrounding wildlife or the meditation hall. It is a smell from before. It is a smell of arriving people, not departing people. I picture black dust rising from him. I picture black dust being churned constantly out of his body.

"Tall. Yes," he says. His accent is heavy. "Do you have transport?" he asks. "I go to Bangkok in taxi. You can join?"

I picture a taxi covered in black dust.

"Thank you," I say. "I have a bus."

He reaches into his pocket and holds a business card out to me.

"I invite you to a restaurant," he says. "Anywhere in the world." I take the card and slip it into my handbag. I can throw it away later.

He nods and waits to see if there is anything else.

"Good to meet you," I say. "Good luck. Goodbye."

I put my hands over my heart. A protective gesture. A blessing. A dismissal.

"Goodbye," he says, and adds, "You are very beautiful."

I do not smile. I turn away.

He walks back through the entrance, towards the dining area and meditation hall, a looming figure. I'm relieved he's gone.

Someone else approaches. The man from the balcony.

"I thought you might need rescuing," he says, tilting his head towards the retreating figure.

"Because I'm a woman?" I ask.

Did I choose that response? No. I fired it back. But, okay. I choose it now. Let's see how he takes it.

He doesn't flinch.

"Because you're in a lovely meditative haze and he looks like he just rolled out of a nightclub."

Not a bad recovery. Humour. He didn't hit back.

"Maybe he was sneaking out to a bar every night?"

"He should have stayed there."

"Mmmm."

"So," the man is saying, "I think before, when we, um, first met..." he pauses to locate his words. "So, I'm usually very careful to make sure that..." He's losing them. "...A lady I'm with is satisfied..."

Aha. I wasn't expecting that.

"So, I have to apologise, because we were interrupted, but if we hadn't been, then I would have made sure that you had, eh, what you needed."

I only realise now that his voice has an accent. Could it be French? It was only a hint. Could I possibly have said *yes* to a Frenchman after...? But wait. My word. *Yes*. It was unconditional. It was unattached. It was free.

He's looking at me. I take the time to select my response.

"It was either that or breakfast," I say. I choose humour. I choose a smile.

He laughs, and I feel relief.

"Mmmmm. Last chance for that mango." He pauses. He opens his hands. "But if there was another time, when you'd, for the sake of argument, choose that over breakfast, well, then I'd be happy to pay back what was owing to you."

I like it. It's courteous. It's unassuming. He's not asking. He's putting it gently on the table, with respect and care. I like it a lot. I like his thoughtfully constructed phrases.

"Do you fly home today?" I ask.

"Yes. London this evening."

"London?" I pause. "Then that should be easy for you to visit me in Paris. I have a café there."

I reach into my bag for the card of my café. Laeticia Montes. Directrice. Café Si La Femme.

"I'll call you in a few days," he says. "Maybe you'll tell me the story of why you were here."

"With some wine."

"That sounds delicious."

"And you can tell me about your *wholeness*."

He laughs. "I'd like that." He pauses. "I'm François," he says. He puts his hand on his heart. I like that too. He does not assume any more physical contact. His respect is beautiful.

"Laeticia," I say.

I see my bus pulling up at the bottom of the steps.

"Good luck, François," I say.

"Good luck," he says. "See you soon."

I sling my bag onto my shoulder and as I pass his body, I slip my fingers into his once more and the jungle weaves through them – our hands – and then we release and I step down the wooden staircase to my bus.

Ivan

Bloody mosquitos.

They were biting me all night.

Tomorrow I'll be in a Bangkok hotel room and I can knock myself out with some vodka. I'll make sure to pick some up on the drive.

I wasn't sure if my blood pressure would go shooting up again yesterday. I waited for the signs: the rush to the head, the buzzing, the faintness. But no. The monk's face in my mind calmed me down. I was able to make clear plans and when my heart started beating too hard, I'd picture the avocado skin, and I'd be tranquil as a Swiss lake.

Four-thirty a.m. We've got to pack and be out by seven. The car is booked and paid for. A few hours to Bangkok and then a luxury hotel. I'll call Eva. I'll call my lawyer. When we arrive I'll go out and get laid.

I'm feeling better already.

I'll never forget the man's face yesterday when I said my word. I could tell he remembered me from the dining room and sobbing in the meditation hall. He knew who I was. His expression was growing more and more scared as I tried to get the word out. It looked as if he thought what I was going to say would make him explode or be like a punch in the stomach. Then I said it – boom! – and his face was horror. He knew it meant death. He knew, as I spoke the word, that it meant someone was going to die. And he was right. What was his word? Oh yes, *return*. I guess he's returning to his inner truth. I imagine Mr. S. N. Goenka will guide him there. He's probably washed his hands of me by now. Find your inner truth? I have done just that, Mr. S. N. Goenka. My inner truth is that I am exactly the man I always have been. I like to fight. I like to win. I like to take. If I have to die for that, then so be it. And if others have to die because I am like that, then it's no different to the jungle. No hard feelings. Nature, my friend. We don't cry about it. We kill, eat and move on.

I've got some unfinished business, though.

A final meditation?

Nice thought, but no.

She's there. Standing at the top of the steps, looking out towards the jungle. I'm amazed I haven't paid more attention to her. She's wearing a hat and a loose dress, but I can see her long body under the fabric. I could take her shopping, buy her clothes to show off her figure. Buy her lingerie. Spread caviar over her.

"Excuse me," I say. I am looking better today. My hair and beard is still overgrown, but I am no longer in my white Adidas suit. Not that I don't look good in it, but now I'm in Ralph Lauren shorts and a blue polo shirt.

She turns. Her face is straight out of a Playboy magazine. Big eyes, smouldering, breasts pushing out through the dress, dark hair.

"I have a car taking me to Bangkok. I wonder if you'd like to share it?" I say. "Unless you have your own means of transportation."

She nods. She looks in my eyes. She's tall. She really could be a magazine model. Not a TV porn star – she's too beautiful for that. You need the rubber-lipped ones for that work. She's not afraid of me and that's a good sign.

"No," she says. "That's a kind offer but I have my own arrangements."

I do not give up. It is not my nature to give up.

"Maybe you would like to meet in Bangkok?" I ask. "I know some very good restaurants."

She is shaking her head.

"Or in Paris?" Every girl likes to go to Paris.

A wall has come down. She doesn't like Paris?

"I don't want to meet you anywhere," she says. She is looking me straight in the eyes. She is not afraid. I read fear professionally and she is not afraid. That leaves me at a disadvantage. Fear gives you an entrance. It makes me want her more, though.

"Let me give you my contact," I say. "If you change your mind, then you should write to me, or call me. We can meet in any city." I hold out my card. "My name is Ivan," I say.

"Pleased to meet you, Ivan." She takes the card. "Good luck with the meditation," she says. "Goodbye."

She turns away. I am confused for a moment about the meditation. It has not occurred to me to continue with it. Perhaps everyone else here will be meditating at four a.m. every morning. Not me. I will be asleep at four a.m. when I get home from the nightclub. Or waking Eva up for a blowjob.

She took the card. I am an optimist. She will get poor and horny. She will remember the tall, rich Ivan who would take her to Paris. Or not Paris. Somewhere else. She will call me.

Now for the last business.

I look in the dining room, but it's being cleared away and there are only servers there. I check on the boardwalk but it's just the meditators looking at the jungle. I walk to the meditation hall. There are a few people in there, one sweeping, one dismantling the video screen and equipment.

He is there. He is standing with the other monks to the side. I approach. He looks up towards me and looks happy. I smile. I put my hand on my heart. He leaves his group of monks. He comes to me. He stands, facing me. We nod and smile. He does the bowing-praying thing. I speak.

"I am Ivan," I say to him, and then I bring my fist back and I punch him in the face and then in the stomach and then in the stomach again. My fist is about the size of his face. It goes in with a satisfying thud. It feels like a virgin face. I'm the first to punch it. It feels good.

He falls over and the other monks come running. I'm done, though. He won't remember any crying and bleeding and praying. He'll remember the punch in the face and the pain and the broken rib. He'll remember that Ivan was a man.

Time to leave.

My bags are ready in reception. I've got my meat back. I'll dig out my aftershave in the car so that I smell like myself again. And there: the car is driving up. I wonder if the monks will chase after it, flapping their orange sheets. I'd love to tell Zhenia the story. I hope I will, one day. Although he'll be dead soon.

There. Mercedes S-Class S-500. Exactly the one I ordered. Things are good. The windows are tinted, there's air conditioning and I'll barely see the jungle through the glass. The driver is waving at me that he'll be back in a moment, he's gone to take a leak.

I'm sure that girl will call. "I'm from the meditation centre in Thailand," she will say. "Yes," I will say, "I am ready to meet. Tell me a city." I'll buy her lingerie and tight clothes and we'll make love for three days in the most expensive hotel in the city. "I love you, Ivan," she'll say. "I love you too, Kitten," I'll say. We'll kiss as I put her on a plane.

Mobile phone. Meat. Aftershave. Razor. Check. Now's the

moment. Switch on the phone. It's taking an age. I wonder if the battery has run down. I leave the bags next to the trunk for the driver, slide onto the back seat and slam the door. Black leather. What a perfect smell. I pull the meat from its packet. It's some Spanish ham, expensive, that I brought from Duty Free. I take a bite. The dead flesh gives me power. I pull out my bottle of aftershave and dab some on. Now I smell like a rich man.

I shake the phone. It's blinking at last. What will it be? A thousand texts? A thousand calls? Let's see. I've got my plan, though. The avocado mirror told me. His eyes met mine and he gave me the idea. It was a well of peace that flooded into my black soul and lit up the radiant deviousness and tangle of angry thoughts into a luminous, clear sequence of inevitable events. Forgiveness. Trust. Intimacy. Safety. And then death. I am the spider. My venom sac is full.

In my head, I'm already back in Kyiv. Eva is waiting for me at the airport. The children are at home. My driver will pick me up in the Maybach. We'll go out to dinner, me and Eva. She'll want to talk. I'll have to explain some things about how it's going to be.

"Don't worry, Rabbit," I'll tell her. "I am better now. All our money is coming back. Don't worry about a thing."

She'll trust me, because she doesn't have any choice. I haven't let her down before.

In Kyiv, the chestnuts will be in bloom.

The phone flashes on.

Text from Eva: Don't get in the car.

Text from Zhenia: Goodbye, brother.

I'd better get out of the car.

and breathe

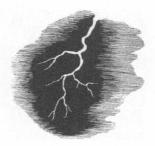

Francis

Boom!
I'm flying through the air.
Flash! Flash! Flash!
A searing noise.
Shouting. Screaming.
Boom!
I've landed.
Pain.
Darkness.
An attack.

I open my eyes. Falling ash. Intense nausea. An aching somewhere in my lower body. I try to raise my hand. The command fails.

My head is reverberating with screams, flames, sickness.

This is my fault. I am trained to anticipate risk. My job is to know when a threat is present. I have failed.

Darkness.

Eyes open.

Through my nausea, I try to activate my analytical skills. One explosion or two? Target? Casualties? Likely weapon? Chance of accident? Number injured (including self)? Personal injury status? Access to medical assistance? Likelihood of ongoing threat to life?

I squint through the ash and smoke. An outline in the distance of a car in flames.

Darkness.

Awake. A searing pain in my lower body. The nausea has become a colour. Intense white. Almost blinding. Swirling grey ash.

This is my fault. I let myself be lulled by the meditation. I relaxed my mental faculties and stepped back into the innocent, unseeing world of oblivion.

This is the result.

Test to raise arm. Fail.

Darkness.

A memory. The farmhouse in Provence. Summer. The stone house. The wooden table in the courtyard with a red-and-white chequered cloth. Carafes of spring water and wine on the lunch table. Maman in a flowered dress and farmyard boots, blonde hair in a plait. Father dressed in Paris casual: loafers and polo shirt. I am in shorts and sandals, walking through the wild grasses around the farmhouse, waiting for lunch to be called. It is hot, I am happy; there is a pile of books next to my bed in French and English that I am permitted to spend my days reading.

In the grass is a grey-green snake. I identify the *Natrix helvetica* by its size and its collar of paler green curving around its throat. It's a female. She's beautiful. I reach down and pick her up carefully as she flicks her black tongue at me. She seems heavier and slower than she should be and I wonder if she has eaten recently.

I carry the snake over to the lunch table. She is a metre long, perhaps one and a half metres. I hold her gently around the throat area and in her middle. She isn't fighting me, she seems to know that I am only interested in her, that I mean no harm.

"Maman, look!" I say in a hushed tone. I don't want to alarm the snake. Maman glances up from arranging the table and her eyes are full of delight.

"What a beauty, Francis!" she exclaims. "Look at her colouring!"

She comes closer and runs her fingers over the immaculate scales. They are dark-grey with a murky green edge, the colour of the faded, cloth-bound books on my bedside shelf in Paris.

"You should draw a picture of her in your journal," Maman says. "Be careful now. Set her down in the grass. It's time for lunch."

Eyes open.

Pain below.

Nausea.

A sudden panic. A vision of the woman – I can't grasp her name – the woman from the balcony – the woman who... – going down the steps to the bus – and the car – and...

Darkness.

Eyes open.

Panic through a haze of half-understandings.

I should have analysed the participants more closely. The robed man in sackcloth. He could have been anyone. I should have looked for more clues. Could he be the attacker? The sobbing giant who pushed a monk in the dining area. The toe-ringed Canadian. Could he have got on the wrong side of drug dealers? I'm certain now it is an attack by a participant. Or *on* a participant. Not the monks or staff. A political attack? Plenty of divisive views in this country. A high-level executive? Meditation courses are popular with powerful people. No bodyguards though. I would have noticed.

There's something I've missed.

My mind catches on to outstretched branches as it drifts back into darkness. Spider. Heat Ray. And then...

My father comes out of the patio door with a platter of cold meats. He sees me holding the long, green-grey snake. His body jerks and his face hardens. He swears at me. He turns back into the farmhouse.

"Quick, put her in the grass," Maman urges, but Papa is already back. He is holding an axe.

I run over to the grass and lay the snake down where she can glide away. Father is behind me. The snake is not moving. "Go! Go!" I tell her.

"Move!" Father pushes me aside and locates the snake.

"Stupid boy," he says to me, his eyes fixed on the grass. "There is enough danger without you bringing snakes into the home."

"But Papa!"

"Leave!"

I step back as he raises the axe and brings it down into the grass. I pray that the snake has gone. I pray that she has glided smoothly into the tall grasses that lead to the river, where she can swim, swim to the other side, swim to her nest, catch a tasty frog for her lunch, exist in her green-grey beauty for as long as the natural world will allow her.

"There." My father's voice. He is walking back towards the farmhouse. I cannot look at the axe.

When he is inside, I run. Past my mother, past her understanding face that makes me want to scream, past the front gate of the driveway and out into the road, then down the road, down the long avenue shaded by elms, down, down, down and deeper into the world, into the dangerous world of snakes and death and axes.

Eyes open. There are tears in them. My vision is swimming and the nausea immediately rises.

This is my fault. Even if I wasn't able to stop this event, I should have been ready for it. The world is dangerous, random, terrifying. It is uncertain. Risk is everywhere. I released my awareness for a single day and I was immediately unprepared.

The searing pain in my leg once again. I should try to get help.

"Hello?" I call out.

No response.

I draw a graph in my head. X axis is my level of awareness to the risks of the surrounding world, from zero – peaceful, meditative trance, to hyper – full paranoid fizzing brain. Y axis shows the percentage likelihood of an attack in the current location.

This took place when the X axis was on zero, and the Y axis was on 100.

A fail.

Go to Thailand, Francis.

You need a break, Francis.

You're seeing things that aren't there, Francis.

Fail.

My father with the axe, eliminating risk.

My father's stone face. *There is enough danger without you bringing snakes into the home.*

Eyes open.

The pain in my leg. Deepest despair in my soul. I have failed. I cannot go forward. I cannot go back. Either I am paranoid or I am blind to real risk. My brain has failed me. My double first has failed me. Jimme has left me. I will have no career. No relationship. No true home.

I try again to sit up.

I struggle and, this time, I can move my torso and one of my arms. I lever my elbow into the ground and push, push, raising myself a few inches. The nausea and dizziness blind me for a moment, but I harden myself to let them pass and then I can look around me.

I am some distance from the meditation centre, perhaps fifty metres. Now I observe what is causing the pain in my leg. A tree has fallen and one of the branches is pinning me. My leg is bent at a strange angle, I suspect it is broken, but it is not the main trunk of the tree lying on me, so it should not be difficult to shift.

The meditation centre appears to be in one piece, however now I see clearly the carcass of a burning car and the wooden stairs destroyed, exposing the foundations of the building. It is an ugly, raw sight. My focus improves as I look around and now I can make out the figures, the people. I'm looking for her. The name still eludes me. It is locked in a part of my brain that has closed down. Fear receptors bolting it shut. I can't see her but I see flashes of orange robes. I look closer, squinting my eyes, and observe two figures embracing. Not moving, just standing with their arms around each other.

And then something strange happens. It is as if a lens has been placed before my eyes – like those at the opticians, to help you read the letters more clearly – but here, I can see not just more clearly, I can suddenly see *more*. Beside the embracing couple, a woman is sitting on the ground with her knees raised, and a monk is kneeling beside her and assisting her. Behind them a man is standing and crying, his body heaving, and a woman is talking to him. I observe that her physical language is supportive and gentle. She is calming him down. Then I look further and in every direction people are touching, embracing, holding, supporting, comforting, aiding, offering, serving, loving. It is as if the Buddha has lent me his own spectacles. I see humanity as I have never seen it before – as it could be, if there was only kindness. As it would be if we loved and served one another. It's the most beautiful thing I've ever seen.

And I realise.

That.

While I was.

Focusing.

Only.

On.

The.

Risk.

That.

This.

Was.

The.

Part.

That.

I.

Missed.

And breathe.

I raise a hand and start waving it towards the wooden building.

"Hello!" I shout. "Hello! I need help!" But it is hard to speak, because I am weeping. I am seeing the couple embracing. I am seeing the monk on his knees. Because there is this, too. There is the goodness also.

The spectacles are blurred with my tears, and I send a silent thank you to the Buddha for lending them to me.

Now, I want more than anything I've ever wanted to be among these people, to share in their service; to help someone if I can. I want more than anything to be in the world, serving, loving, assisting.

I will choose this. I must choose it. I will hold on to this. I will hold on to the thought of a cup of coffee in Paris, where there is the best coffee in the world. A tiny cup, a spring morning, a seat outside, a bad-tempered lady feeding morsels to a pampered dog, a tall, graceful woman beside me. She has short, dark hair and golden skin. The taste of coffee, a shudder of bitterness, she takes my hand. It is all love.

"François?"

I look up. She is there. She is alive. Her name comes to me. Laeticia. Her eyes are caring. Her eyes are warm. She will be waiting for me in Paris.

"I'm quite alright," I say. Even though my leg is pinned by a tree. Even though there has been a violent attack on our meditation centre. Even though I clearly cannot move.

In fact, for the first time in a long, long while, I feel joy.

I give a little laugh. I hope it doesn't come across as that silly, self-deprecating thing the English do. It's a genuine laugh. She'll think I'm mad. I don't care. It just doesn't matter.

I feel her eyes on me.

"I'm quite alright."

ACKNOWLEDGMENTS

Thank you to everyone who helped me with the creation of this book, from Galyna, who first told me about Vipassana in a café on Lesi Ukraina Boulevard in Kyiv, to the writing group at Richmond Library in London who liked the first page; Melody, who shared her Thailand meditation experiences with me – unfortunately your scorpion didn't make it in – and my beta readers Kate, Herb, Kathleen and Diana. Thank you to Dan for loving it from the start, to Anna Green for another beautiful cover, and to Valentina for being uncompromising in her demand for fairness and equality in the world. Thank you to all the readers who told me in confidence that they loved Ivan the best; I'm sure his afterlife is filled with caviar and expensive cars.

Thank you also to readers of my earlier books who have supported me on the writing journey. It's a small miracle every time you learn that something you spent years of your life on was worth it.

Teddington

January 2022

THE WOMAN BEHIND THE WATERFALL

"A LITERARY WORK OF ART" – RICHMOND MAGAZINE

Magic and transformation in the beauty of a Ukrainian village

For seven-year old Angela, happiness is exploring the lush countryside around her home in western Ukraine. Her wild imagination takes her into birds and flowers, and into the waters of the river.

All that changes when, one morning, she sees her mother crying. As she tries to find out why, she is drawn on an extraordinary journey into the secrets of her family, and her mother's fateful choices.

Can Angela lead her mother back to happiness before her innocence is destroyed by the shadows of a dark past?

Beautiful, poetic and richly sensory, this is a tale that will haunt and lift its readers.

THE UNITY GAME

A "MIND-BENDING SCI-FI SAGA THAT STRETCHES ACROSS TIME AND SPACE!" - BOOKBUB

What if the Earth you knew was just the beginning?

A New York banker is descending into madness.

A being from an advanced civilization is racing to stay alive.

A dead man must reveal the secrets of a new dimension to save his loved ones.

Can these characters see through the game to the ultimate reality and transform everything they have ever known, before life on Earth plummets into a hellish nightmare?

From the visions of Socrates in ancient Athens, to the birth of free will aboard a spaceship headed to Earth, *The Unity Game* tells a story of wonder and discovery in a universe more ingenious and surprising than you ever thought possible.

With this metaphysical thriller, author Leonora Meriel "leaves you questioning everything you know" - **Goodreads reviewer**

MBAQUANGA NIGHTS

"A WILD RIDE THAT STRETCHES THROUGH JAZZ AND HISTORY" - ZOE MCLEOD

1989.

The African Jazz Pioneers are in full swing. Coltrane's club is hopping. Glasses and plates are pushed aside as the room dances.

What's so special?

Look around. The faces are black, brown and white. It's Durban, South Africa. It's apartheid. It's illegal.

When a pair of young music lovers decide to follow their dreams and open a jazz club to host their favourite musicians, they have little idea of what stark choices they will be facing as the political situation heats up and riots tear through the surrounding townships.

With an epic tale that starts in the depths of a Ukrainian shtetl and winds its way back and forth across oceans, history and memory serve to create a personal story of individual choice – and the fate of nations.

Available from November 2022